BitterSweet

By

Allison

"Essence M"

Edwards

The following is a work of fiction. Characters, names, situations, events, and locations described in this novel are purely the invention of the author's mind, or are used fictitiously. Any sort of resemblance to people - living or dead, names and locations is purely coincidental. Any references to real people, events, establishments or locales are intended only to give the fiction a sense of reality and authenticity. This story is copyrighted and cannot be taken or displayed without the expressed written permission of the author.

Library of Congress Control Number: 2011961704

ISBN-10: 0983048126

ISBN-13: 978-0983048121

Cover Concept and Design by Illuminnessence Publishing

www.illuminnessencepublishing.com

Edited by Brandie Randolph / brandie@editingcouture.com

www.editingcouture.com

For all orders and inquiries, please contact illuminnessencepub@gmail.com

Forever The Hustla- Chasing The Diamonds!!

Other titles available include:

"Broken Promises Never Mend"

"Bound By Lies"

Dedication-

To Elletina Adina Buckley &

Ivy Mae Edwards,

Two of the strongest women I know aside from my mother, Grace!

I Love You!

Acknowledgements

GOD- I was raised to place you first and you never know how much that means until you are tested. I thank YOU and give you honor for all I have yet to see.

My family (Mommy, Daddy, Bro & Sister) has been there for me this whole journey and I love and thank you for it from the bottom of my heart. I don't know where I'd be without your constant support and encouragement.

My sons, I do it ALL for you! I love you both with all my heart!

To my friends, thank y'all for riding this out with me. I am never out of touch or too far away to forget you all. I am and always will be simply "ALLIE"

To all my author friends that I've made along the way, you all have helped me so much (some more than others)- It would be unfair of me to personally name you all but know you all have inspired me to be better in so many ways. Extra special love goes out to Erick Gray, Victoria Christopher Murray, Julia Press Simmons, K'wan, Nakea Murray, Treasure Blue, T. Styles , Charisse Washington and the entire Cartel Publications

To My Editor- Brandie Randolph of Editing Couture--Once again you have done it and given my words life. I appreciate all you do for me! Fabulosity at its finest! <3

To my fans/supporters, I appreciate all the love you have given me as a newbie and I hope that you will continue to follow my journey. It's only the beginning of a journey that I plan to continue! Whoever I "forgot", please know I love you still-Charge It To My Head and Not My Heart!

Much Love Always

A Note from the Author

Here we are again and I am so pleased that you have chosen to indulge once again, another one of my novels. Ever since I released my first and second novels (respectively) "Broken Promises Never Mend" & "Bound by Lies", I've seen things so differently. The friends I thought I had were nowhere to be found and the ones that I discounted as such have been some of my biggest supporters.

This book chronicles a woman's journey to chase the very thing that is her motive for escape. You can't run from who you are. You will always be reminded of the path and it's up to you to adapt.

I hope you all enjoy this as it is unrelated to my other two novels yet is so different and in my opinion unique that you can't help but understand the decisions made and why. It also touches areas that are considered taboo in the community. I thank you all once again for joining me and I pray this entertains you, enlightens you and encourages you in some way to go for your dream. Many of you have asked me to help you get started on your novels. It's within you. Begin and don't stop!

Love you all to pieces and Thank you!

Allison "Essence M" Edwards

Official Website:

www.illuminnessencepublishing.com

Email:

illuminnessencepub@gmail.com

Table of Contents

Bittersweet

- **Bottom Bitch**

- **Home is Where The Heart Is**

- **The Rotten Apple**

- **Watch the Throne**

- **Sweet Vengeance**

Bittersweet

My Prerogative

A juicy gob of spit dripped down her chin. Brianna had never done this at work before, but as soon as he mentioned he would pay extra for private service, she decided to go for it. Frankly speaking – "what the fuck!" Women have been giving up pussy for years without being compensated for it. It's time to get paid for services rendered!

Her hand moved up and down the shaft of his erect penis as she kept it in her mouth. He groaned and grunted in pleasure while Brianna sucked on his dick like a Hoover vacuum. The throbbing in her mouth was felt as it bobbed and remained warm and wet causing her to taste his pre cum. Brianna knew he was about to blow his wad down her throat and was ready to keep sucking and stroking until he did.

Brianna said she would only do this when she was in a relationship but lately, she was tired of being mistreated for where she worked and how she made her money. Any man that wanted to be with her would have to know and understand that Brianna was an exotic dancer or a plain ol' stripper and this is how she made her money. The Golden Palace was a place where friends and foes were made on a daily basis. Every man/woman and child for themselves and no one was exempt from being a target, no matter who you were.

Brianna began to hum so that the back of her throat massaged his dick and tickled the tip. She was determined to keep her mouth wet because Brianna decided she wasn't going to fuck him. That was really the last resort. This man was as big as a house, about 350 lbs. and smelled like stale Newport cigarettes and Heineken beer.

His sweaty belly kept hitting her in the face when she changed positions and she felt the prickly hairs on his crotch rub her hands as she grabbed and massaged his dick.

Brianna wanted to get this over with so she could get her dough and finish her shift. One more hour was left on her shift for the night and she wanted to get home to rest up for her other job as a Home Health Aide. She hated that she had to have two jobs, but it was the only way she could legitimize why she couldn't finish school when she was supposed to.

Financial aid ran out and she had to take a semester off, but that was a year ago and now she's stuck stripping by night and nursing by day. She was determined to move out of the projects if it killed her. Way too many things occurred and she was beginning to be fearful for her life. Living at home wasn't an easy task either and that's another reason why she remained at work.

With the task at hand and money being the motive, she focused back at her client and sucked harder in order to speed up his process. He grabbed the back of her dark brown hair and began to fuck her face hard and fast, causing her to gag. He knew he wasn't going to get the pussy, so her tongue was the next best thing. Brianna had her 42DDs out of her purple bikini top and he played with her nipples asshe knelt between his legs, going to work on his chocolate penis.

"Uh, yeah, ooh, take this dick! Ooh damn! I'm gonna cum!"he said, as she took her mouth off and let him bust his jizz all over her tits. She was supposed to swallow but, at the last minute, decided against it, moving her mouth off of his penis and allowing it to ejaculate the sticky white fluid on her breasts.

"That's a dumb move, bitch!" he said, wiping the tip of his dick with a baby wipe and pulling his pants above what should be his waist, but his big gut hung over. He struggled to buckle the belt and just left it dangling which made it jingle when he walked.

"This is why they call it 'VIP' and you didn't treat me like a very important person!" He pulled out his wallet and began to count out three single hundred dollar bills. They were crisp and rustled as he did, so he licked his fingertips and used the saliva to separate the sticky bills.

"This is why they call it 'prerogative'. Just run me my money so I can tend to my other clients. I got shit to do." Brianna adjusted her bra top and grabbed some baby wipes to clean her mouth and chest, which was dripping in his ejaculate. She didn't want her next client to know she did this or else they'd all want it and, while he was her first, she didn't particularly care for it.

Besides going home to her mom's house, she didn't want to smell like sex. Smelling like old people was bad enough and she did that every day to pay the bills. Stripping was for extra shit she wanted and she didn't intend to stop until she got what she wanted.

"You know I give two fucks, right? I just did you a favor, so give me what's owed to me and I'll be on my way." Her mouth was slick and she knew how to make people give her what she wanted. Brianna stuck a piece of gum in her mouth and re-applied her ruby red lipstick. She stuck her hand out for payment and waited patiently for him to give her the money owed. He placed it in her hand and he smirked. She counted the money and rolled her eyes.

"This isn't all my money," she responded, realizing that he shorted her $200 for a job half done. It wasn't what was agreed upon and she kind of wished silently that she did what he wanted.

"It's my prerogative, remember?" he said as he kissed her on the cheek and walked through the curtains. He looked back and said, "Next time, do what you are supposed to do and you'll get all that you want."

"Shit!" she exclaimed as she threw the money on the rust colored sofa in the VIP section of the club. Another fucked up night at the club, but it gave her an idea that would change her life forever.

| Bittersweet

Home Sweet Home

Walking out of the subway on 125th Street, Brianna Thomas felt like she was taking the "Walk of Shame". You know, the walk that one takes at 6AMwhen you leave a nigga's house that you have been fucking on the low. Her duffel bag was slung over her shoulder and her face was fresh and free of makeup after last night's shift at the Golden Palace. She hated the fact that she had to come home at this time, but it was a blessing as well as a curse.

"Watch where the fuck you are going!" said a man who bumped into her with his briefcase. He was clearly in a hurry and didn't even look back to see if she was okay. She rolled her eyes as she viewed him running down the stairs to catch the train. *New Yorkers are always in a rush,* she thought, but they were always in a rush to get money; a sentiment she could identify with all too well.

Brianna crossed the street and tried to figure out what she was going to eat before she got home because she knew that would help her sleep for tonight's shift at her other job. She lucked out that this job was 3 PM to 10 PM because her nights as a stripper at the Golden Palace began at roughly midnight until 4AM. By the time she was ready to go home, the rest of the world was ready to go to work to make their money.

Brianna stepped into the local West Indian Bakery, "Taste the Island" to grab a beef patty and coco bread along with some bun and cheese. She wasn't Jamaican, but loved the way the food coated her stomach after a night of drinking and smoking weed. It was a definite relief to have some good food in her stomach since she didn't get that at home.

She paid for her food and her hand touched the male cashier slightly. He smiled at her as if he knew her. She smiled politely and adjusted the strap on her duffel bag which was hung by her hips. She was used to him being polite since she visited the spot about twice a week. He usually hooked her up with an extra bun and cheese or cola champagne and today was no different. She winked at him and began to head to her least favorite place ever: home.

Brianna walked up the street to her block and pulled her coat closer to her. Her black North Face coat was no match for her body which rivaled Rosa Acosta. Her long, flowing, ebony hair was in a neat ponytail that cascaded down the middle of her back. Her House of Dereon jeans and Nine West boots gave her a swag that made her believe she owned the world. Her hazel eyes with hints of gold in glistened in the sun. She arrived at her brownstone on 122nd

Street and Lenox and took a deep sigh. She hated coming home to drama but lately, that's all she knew.

Brianna trotted reluctantly up the steps and put the key in the door. It was then she heard what she was getting tired of each and every day.

"You fucking whore! I know you are spending up all my fucking money on shit you don't need. I'm tired of coming home and seeing you with some new shit, knowing good and well you don't need it. Who are you trying to impress?"

It was her mother's boyfriend, Herman. He worked in the day as a maintenance man for a few buildings in the Bronx and lived there occasionally, providing liquor and smoke. Brianna's mother met him three years ago and brought him home like a stray dog. She was first introduced to him at the age of 17 and he had been nothing but trouble ever since.

"Shut the fuck up, you asshole! I slave at night to make sure you can sleep in my muthafuckin' bed and have food when you come home to me, and this is the thanks I get? You drink all my Henny and smoke all my trees and don't even fuck me like I want anymore. Look, fuckboy! When you can provide me with the things I need, then you can say shit."

That was her mother, Ophelia Thomas, but the block called her Fifi. She's been living in Harlem, New York for 25 years and everyone knows her name. It's been considered both a blessing and a curse. Ophelia was one of those MILFs that everyone talks about. She's 5'2" and her skin is a caramel complexion, just like Brianna's. Her hair is auburn colored and shoulder length. Her nose is as straight as a pin and her eyes are black like charcoals from the

13

fireplace. Her shape resembles a Coca Cola bottle and her ass was passed down to her daughter. Her mother is not one of those women to be played with. She's 39 years old and doesn't look a day over 25. Her sex appeal has brought men to their knees on many occasions and this time would be no different.

"Fifi, you keep spending up all my money and I'm getting tired of it! Let me give that shit to you. The fuck you going in my pockets for?"

"Nigga, you in MY house! I do what the fuck I want! Next time I find an empty condom wrapper in my bed, I'ma slice ya fucking throat. Do you hear me?"

Fifi was feisty and no match for Herman's strength which had him towering over her at 6'1" and 230lbs. He lunged towards her and grabbed her by the throat, holding her against the wall with one hand. Her feet dangled off the floor and she gasped for air.

"Herbie, please! Baby! I'm sorry! I didn't mean to talk to you that way! You know you are my #1. Just don't let them bitches leave their shit here is all," Fifi said, barely above a whisper. It was clear that as much mouth that she had a few minutes ago, Herman ran things and let her believe she had the upper hand.

"Fuck with me again and you will have a permanent imprint in this wall! You hear me, Ophelia?" Herman said, spitting venom with his tongue and his tone. He put her down gently and turned toward the front door where Brianna saw everything.

"Hey, ma! You good?" Brianna walked into the living room and picked up a picture of her and her mom that fell off the wall during their violent melee.

15

"Hey, Bri! Yea, I'm okay," she said, readjusting her ponytail and her disheveled clothes.

Brianna looked over at Herman and he winked at her. She knew she would see him alone eventually and she wasn't looking forward to it. He had harassed her daily for so long, but never got to do what he wanted to do. If Brianna told her mother, she would only accuse her of stealing her boyfriend, much like Fifi did a few years back to Brianna.

Ricardo Graham was Brianna's first boyfriend and, at the age of 19, he was everything she thought a man would be. She was only 15 years old and, while she was in school and realizing her sexuality, Ricardo knew it already and wanted it all to himself. Sadly, Fifi knew about it, too, and she knew her daughter couldn't satisfy a sexually charged young man like him, so she seduced him.

16

Brianna came home to find Ricardo in bed with her mother and she cried herself to sleep that night. She ended it and blamed it on the fact that she wanted to preserve her virginity and he wasn't the one. He didn't seem to care anyway since he was fucking Fifi. Fifi knew that Brianna had found out ,but blamed it on the Vodka she indulged in daily.

"Hey, Brianna!" Herman said, looking at her as she removed her coat revealing her dark blue cable knit turtleneck sweater which made her breasts look bigger than ever.

"Hey, Herman! How are you?" Brianna hated small talk with him because it always ended up being perverse and borderline X-rated.

Brianna hung her coat in the hallway closet and walked over to the table in the kitchen to get a glass of soda to drink with her food that she bought earlier. She couldn't wait to get into

17

her pajamas. Herman watched Brianna's every move and grabbed her bag of food before she was able to retreat to her room.

"You know ya momma don't like eating in your room. It breeds rats and roaches." He slowly opened the bag and took out a piece of bun and cheese and placed it in his mouth. She began to feel flushed with anger as he didn't take his eyes off of her the whole time, knowing it would anger her. He would end up eating it all from her, leaving her with nothing if she didn't stop him soon.

"If my momma is worried about pests then why the fuck does she keep you around?" Brianna spat back and grabbed the bag from him, but not before he grabbed her wrist and pulling her close.

"You watch your mouth, little girl! I'm old enough to be your father!" Herman was really angry and tried to bully Brianna just like he bullied Fifi but the difference was, Brianna wasn't scared of him. She felt like he had nothing to hold over her head.

"Nigga, are you crazy? My father wouldn't ever disrespect me like you have and he damn sure wouldn't ever disrespect my mother. You need to go 'head with that bullshit and leave me the hell alone. You and I have no business here and I have to go to work later." Brianna snatched her hand back from him and began to walk away.

"You think I don't know what you do? You think I don't see you shake your fat ass at the Golden Palace? I'm there at least once a month, and my friends see you also. That little wig and costume you wear sometimes doesn't do shit. I know Fifi, and I know you. You have a sexy little body there." Herman grabbed her hair out of the ponytail and began to inhale it sneakily.

Brianna's heart began to race as she wondered if he would tell her mother what she's been up to in her spare time. Her mother just thinks she's been working double shifts as a home health aide. As long as she's giving Fifi money for Hennessy and weed, she was okay, but she was still worried that Fifi would find out because that means she had more money than she was giving and was stashing it.

"What the fuck do you mean you see me? You know where I work, so don't even try to tell me..." Brianna began her tirade but was cut off abruptly by Herman's loud booming voice.

"You and your little sassy ass work at the Golden Palace! I even tipped you $20 one night last week and I heard you gave my coworker,

Jeremy, a mean blow job! Is THAT how you are making tips now?" Herman blew her cover and left Brianna speechless.

Bittersweet

What's Done in the Dark

Brianna placed the bag of food in her hand on the counter and looked at Herman. His smirk said it all- he had something to hold over her head and would make her life miserable if she didn't comply. She hated him even more now but this would cause her to play his game if need be. She was used to playing games but, with him, it would be like playing Chess and staying ahead of him us the ultimate goal in order to win.

"Okay, okay... I will admit it. I work at the Golden Palace. Did you see me? Did you like what you saw? Why didn't you speak so I could give you a private show? You know you think of me when you fuck my mother!" Brianna began to antagonize him and discovered she liked this game more and more. She lowered her hand, caressing his crotch which grew with arousal.

Herman's forehead developed beads of sweat and he lost his voice momentarily. He had to regain his composure since Brianna began mind-fucking him.

"I.... I... I don't think of you when I'm with your mother. What kind of person do you think I am?"

"I know exactly what kind of person you are and if you keep your mouth shut, then you will get some extra shit from me. If not, then all bets are off. One hand will wash the other. Deal?"

"What kind of extra shit are you talking? There's only one thing that I want from you and that's priceless as far as I am concerned. 'Til I get that, nothing else will matter," Herman said, licking his lips seductively.

Brianna knew what she would have to give up in order to make him be quiet, but she decided to keep it monetary.

"I'll give you an extra $250 a month so that you can continue to do what you have to do outside of my mother without worrying she's skimming from your stash. How's that?"

Herman pulled a Newport cigarette out of his pocket, along with a lighter, and inhaled the smoke. He was skeptical of their deal, but he felt she had so much more to lose so he agreed. He was tired of Fifi spending all the money he had for recreation to satisfy her own selfish needs. He wanted Brianna to compensate for his losses and help him out.

"That's fine. It'll be our little secret. My lips will be sealed." Herman walked over to her and gave her a sloppy kiss on the forehead just as Fifi was walking in to view the exchange.

"What the hell is this bullshit that I see? Since when are you and Herbie best fucking friends?" Fifi was slurring her words and clearly drunk. She sat in the living room and drank Vodka to numb the pain she was experiencing. It took her all of 20 minutes to begin to feel the effects, especially since she hadn't really eaten anything all day.

"Momma, Herbie and I are cool. We just had a misunderstanding and we've cleared it up. We are cool now; not friends, but not besties. I'm tired now and going to take a nap so I can get ready to work my double tonight." Brianna looked at Herman to see if he would hint to her real whereabouts but the payoff was sweet enough to silence him.

She walked down the hallway with food and drink in hand and entered her room to finally relax. It was already almost nine o'clock in the morning and she hadn't slept yet. First thing she did was remove her clothing. She hated sleeping in clothes and pulled off her jeans, sweater and boots. Briana hung up her clothes and took a look at herself in her full length mirror. No wonder men are willing to pay good money to see her dance and then get serviced after.

Brianna sat on her bed Indian style and began to finally dig into her meal. Her washboard stomach was exposed as she dug into the meal that would probably be the only one she'd have all day. She enjoyed this quiet time and turned it to the **BET** network to unwind and relax. One of her favorite songs came on the screen and it was Keri Hilson's *Pretty Girl Rock*.

Brianna thought about her outward beauty and knew that it was so alluring that she would be able to turn anyone into a **YES MAN**. It has worked in the past and still works in her profession as a stripper. She finished eating and tossed her garbage in the can by her bedroom door and began to watch the video. The moves that they were dancing to could definitely be used in tonight's performance. She began to sway her hips back and forth and her body moved seductively to the music. Brianna was a very developed young woman and her breasts grew at an astonishing pace from the time she was 11 years old.

She loved her body and did her best to keep it in tip top shape. Feeling tired and ready to rest, she lay in her bed and her mind began to wander. She felt herself getting comfortable and began to touch herself. Brianna placed her hands in her black lace Victoria's Secret bra and pulled on her nipples, causing them to stand at attention.

There was no better feeling than knowing that you turned yourself on without having to worry about a man doing it. While her left hand began tugging at her caramel mounds, her right hand descended below to slip her matching lace panties to the side. They were already wet with arousal after thinking about all the naughty things she would do later on tonight.

Reaching under the bed, she pulled out her goody bag with her silver bullet. She was going to make herself fall asleep with a smile on her face one way or the other. With the melodic sounds of BET as her backdrop, she turned on her pleasuring toy and placed it on her clit that was already tense with arousal and peeking its head out from the hood of her pussy. It began to vibrate and hum a tune that made her tingle and moan softly. Opening herself wider so that she can feel more, she placed the bullet damn near inside of her pussy.

"Mmmmmmmm Ooooooooooo," was all that could be heard from her room. Her bed became a mess as she began secreting juices from her dripping labia. She felt some on her fingers and tasted it. It just made her more aroused because she knew what pussy tasted like. She'd had experienced bisexuality a time or two at the job. She loved dick too much to be a lesbian, but knowing that this feeling was what other women felt when she licked, sucked and nibbled their pussy made her want to explode in ecstasy. It had been a while since she had that craving, but she didn't mind. She was all about the money nowadays and was channeling Rick Ross' song *Money Makes Me Cum*.

Over and over, she inserted the miniature dick inside of her and writhed in pleasure on the bed. Soon enough, the throbbing became too much to bear and she climaxed right there on the bed and squirted her tasty treats as evidence of her escape to erotic bliss. She couldn't believe she held in so much liquid and her bed was soaked to the mattress. She grabbed her robe and threw it on so she could go to the bathroom and retrieve a towel to clean up. When she did, she bumped smack into Herbie who had his dick out of his pants with the same towel in his hand underneath it. He had been watching her and jerked off on her towel.

"What the fuck are you doing? Why do you have my towel, you sick fuck?" Brianna lost her breath momentarily and was annoyed to find him hanging out around her room. She didn't know what was more embarrassing; him using her towel or him using her as his personal XXX rated peep show.

"Come on! You didn't think I'd not want to see what you were doing in there? You were awfully loud! I watched the whole thing and, boy, do you know how to work a vibrator. Do you know how to work a dick, too?" Herbie was full of tricks today and was determined to push her buttons.

31

"Did you like what you saw? I hope so because that's the last time you will ever see anything without paying the appropriate price! I don't work for free. Get the fuck out of my way!"

The linen closet was her next destination before heading back to her room and going to bed. She remembered this time to lock the door and, after attempting to relax yet again, drifted off into a deep slumber to continue yet another day of work. The more things changed, the more they stayed the same but one day soon, the monotony would change in more ways than one.

You Get What You Pay For

The next couple of weeks, Brianna and Herman kept their interaction as normal but it was agreed upon that she go meet him in the Bronx once a week and give him "lunch" in a paperbag. It was actually his idea and he had Fifi cosign since she wouldn't be able to do it due to work.

"But, momma, I hate getting on that bus. It's so damn long and I don't want to be late for work!" Brianna whined, hoping her mother would have a change of heart and do it herself. She wasn't about to risk making this a habit because then, the more Herman saw from her, he would want from her. You know how niggas are! Give them an inch and they take two miles!

"Why can't you do what the fuck I ask you to do? I don't ask for much, but your slick ass mouth just won't comply for once in ya muthafuckin' life! Always talkin' slick and then thinking when people see you they will do what you want!" Fifi had it with her mouth and wanted to make her feel guilty. It was working, but Brianna had something else in mind.

"Ma, I give money and drinks to you quite often but, because I don't want to be late and I want to get this over with, I'm going to do it. Give me the bag so I can go and make it to work on time."

"That's my baby! Now, did you leave money for me? You know the rent is paid for by my SSI and ain't enough for us to live."

"Yes, Momma. I left 100 on the dresser for you along with a pack of Newports. I'll see you later, okay?" Brianna grabbed the bag and her duffle bag containing her uniforms for the night. She was kind of excited because she was going to see her best friend at work. She loved hanging out with Cathleen "Cookie" Richards. They always had so much fun together and they both had a goal; to get the fuck out of the projects and move to where they could pursue their dreams of fame.

She hopped into the subway at 125th Street and got on the express train to the Bronx to give Herman what was coming to him. She wished she had more to give him but, for now, this would have to do until she could give him what he was owed. Taking the subway always brought about fond memories of her and her mother and without fail, she always saw a mother and child interacting in a way she wishes that she did with her own mother.

Fifi and Brianna weren't estranged. They just didn't have a good relationship after Brianna's father left. Fifi began to drink and smoke and not care at all. She injured herself at work and was diagnosed with clinical depression.

She was eligible for Social Security benefits and Section 8 and was able to stay home. Fifi used that to her advantage and began milking the city of New York for all it would give her. Brianna hated covering up for her mother and lying to her teachers about her home life. Nights of keeping Fifi from hurting herself and going to find her off the streets when she was drunk began to ruin her education and she almost didn't graduate from high school.

One teacher, Ms. Moore, had faith in Brianna and her senior year in high school was able to pass all her classes with assistance and she was granted a partial scholarship to Manhattan Community College. Sadly, Brianna dropped out after her first year because her mother almost overdosed on prescription pills. Fifi had become like a child while Brianna was the provider in many aspects and it was overwhelming and strained the relationship they had. It would never be the same again.

Brianna exited at her train stop and waited to transfer to the bus to take the package to Herman. She hated where he worked and didn't like seeing some of the men she saw at her other job in the daylight. She preferred seeing the money they had in their hand as opposed to the persons carrying it. All of a sudden, while waiting for the bus, Brianna was startled by a white Escalade with the bass blaring and music by Drake vibrating through the speakers that drove into the bus stop so quickly it caused Brianna to say,

"Watch where the fuck you are going, you damn psycho!" Brianna yelled at the tinted windows, not caring that she didn't know who it was. The mystery driver rolled down the window and Brianna's face began to flush with arousal and embarrassment.

"Yo, ma, I'm sorry. Your beauty hypnotized me and I wanted to get your attention so I could talk to you," he said.

"Yeah, okay. It's cool, but you don't have to kill me in the process." Brianna adjusted her zipper nervously on her coat and undid her scarf to allow more air because this man had her feeling some sort of way and she didn't even know why.

"No, really. I saw you when you came off the train and walked across the street. I have an appointment in Hunts Point and I wanted to talk to you before you got away from me." The driver rolled down his window more and Brianna lost her breath immediately.

"Whassup, tho'? I'm Antoine, but the streets call me Rico. Are you from around here?" he said, grabbing the handle to the car door motioning her to get inside.

"Wassup, Antoine? I'm Brianna, but the streets call me Honey."Brianna laughed as she said that because she never did have a street name. She just did that to seem more hardcore. She would end up using that name soon to re-invent herself at work.

"Look, Honey, I gotta get out the bus lane. Come with me and I'll take you where you need to go. The bus is coming and you being so sexy is about to cost me $55 for blocking traffic." Antoine looked behind him at the oncoming traffic and the bus that was approaching and honking furiously.

Brianna looked at the angry bus driver and made a quick decision to jump in the car and they sped off, beginning a friendship that would soon develop into something more but cause her to have to choose sides if she wasn't careful.

"So, where am I taking you, Honey?" Antoine inquired, as he entered the Bruckner Expressway ramp to handle his business for the day.

"Oh, yeah, I just need to drop something off on Lafayette Avenue near Story Avenue."

Brianna held the package closely which contained Herman's lunch and dessert (money in a Tupperware container) to hand over to him as hush money. Antoine took a closer look at Brianna and she was just the type of woman he was looking for. She was young, sexy and seemed to not give a fuck when it came to business.

He was right to an extent, but what he wasn't aware of was she was out for self. No one mattered to her; not when the sole purpose of her fucking with Herman was to escape the confines of Harlem and move someplace where she could essentially start over. Her secrets were held deep within her heart and would remain there until said time.

Antoine noticed Brianna in deep thought and while parked at a stop light, he asked her again what was in the bag.

"Yo, ma! You holding on to that shit kinda tight. You got some kinda gold stashed in there or something?" Antoine laughed, but Brianna giggled nervously. She shook the thermos containing Herman's favorite drink in there so the contents would be thoroughly mixed. He loved ice tea but hated for the sugar to rest at the bottom. He'd gotten mad at Fifi for that once and smacked her so hard, he busted her bottom lip.

"Nah, everything is cool. Thank you so much, Rico, for the ride and I don't know if I'll see you again, but I appreciate it. Now I won't be late for work." Brianna opened the car door and was about to exit and walk away when Antoine touched her hand.

"Honey, call me if you need me again. I'm serious. I don't want you to get in any trouble. but if you can get away. I wanna see you and hang out for real. Lemme know."

Brianna took the card and placed it in her pocket. She had less than an hour to get to work and wanted to get there and talk to her friend about some things that were going down. Things were about to change drastically for everyone in her life.

She walked up the ramp into the building and asked to speak to Herman. The security guard eyeballed her up and down and licked his lips.

"What the hell are you looking at? You ain't neva seen a bitch before? You need to chill for real before I snatch your eyes outta your head while you're standing there drooling like a fucking retard!"

"Mr. Wilson will be with you shortly. Please have a seat." he said shaking his head at her display of attitude.

Herman came downstairs within minutes and walked over to Brianna. She couldn't be more pleased, especially because she'd have to take a cab to the club if he made her late. She wasn't happy to see him, but made it pleasurable for the sake of appearances.

"Hey, Herbie! Momma asked me to drop off your lunch today and I put a lil' slice of dessert in there for you. I hope you are satisfied with it. You'll only get it once a week." Brianna was obviously referring to the money, but the security guard was so into the conversation that she had to replace fact with code words.

"Thank you and I'll be sure to enjoy the tasty treat you left me." Herman smirked at Brianna knowingly.

"I'm quite sure you will. Oh, I almost forgot...this is something a little extra for you!" Brianna handed Herman the thermos of iced tea for him to drink on his lunch hour.

"Oh, for me as well? You are too kind!" Herman opened up the thermos, took a huge gulp of the drink, and wiped his mouth, saving the rest for lunch time.

"Okay, well, I'll talk to you later!" Brianna smiled and walked away. She hailed down a cab and used $30 to take her to the outskirts of Mount Vernon, New York where she would live the life that allows her to escape the bullshit she called her reality. She arrived at work and smiled knowing that the end will soon justify the means.

A Plan in Motion

Brianna walked into the Golden Palace and headed straight to the locker room. She bumped into "Bear", the bouncer that always looked out for her during the nights that she left late.

"Hey, Bear! How are things tonight? We gon' make some money or will I be struggling for peanuts?" I said as I surveyed the club for some regulars and also some new meat. I had to hit them first and give them my best moves and hopefully move them to VIP for some more of what I did earlier this week.

"Yeah, Bri, there are some thirst buckets in here tonight. Do I need to man VIP again?" Bear asked, knowing Brianna was on to something that would probably be continuous while she stacked her money to get the hell outta dodge.

"Oh yeah, Bear, you can definitely stand guard for me. You got me for 100, right?" Brianna smiled, knowing that while he would want more maybe, just maybe she would also bless him with some head.

"A'ight, Brianna, I got you." Bear walked away with a smile on his face, looking like Yogi Bear when he lands a picnic basket filled with treats.

Now to change and get my hustle on, Brianna thought to herself.

"Bitch, I know you ain't just gonna walk in and not speak!"It was Cookie, her best friend and she's so lucky that it was her that referred to her as bitch. The last girl that worked here and called Brianna out of her name lost an eye when a heel accidentally on purpose connected with it. Raven consequently learned her lesson and was never heard from again.

"Hey, hoe! I heard there's some niggas out there that look like they got some money! You are just the person I wanted to see. I have a proposition for you and it could make us up to one thousand dollars each! Are you down?"

Cookie loved the idea already. All she really had to hear was dollar signs and she lit up. She wasn't a pretty girl but she had a body that rivaled Melyssa Ford in her prime. Cookie had dark brown skin and long hair. People usually paid her compliments like 'you are very pretty to be so dark'. She hated that and working at the Golden Palace she realized no one really worried about her complexion. They just worried about the ass she was shaking in front of them. If they were willing to pay, she was willing to forget about who she was and take on another identity.

"What the fuck you mean, you have a proposition for me? I mean, I'm down, but I still need to know what I'm getting into. I ain't gonna get killed or nothing, right? I got my son to live for."

Cookie sat on the bench in the locker room and picked her nail polish off nervously. She was already dressed for the night and usually did her set after Brianna. Tonight she was supposed to work with her so she had time to relax and chill and even smoke a blunt.

"Okay, Cookie, don't ask me shit 'bout you getting killed. Why would I even get you mixed up in something like that? I look like a dummy? I just wanna give you and Tyrell a little something more to look forward to for the holiday season. Now, I know I did something the other day and it was worth five notes. I didn't even do what I was supposed to but that's cool with me. Now what I want to do is more and if you follow my lead, we will be just fine. Deal?"

Brianna looked at Cookie and saw her questions in her eyes and smiled. Cookie was so naïve at times even though she was a bit older. That's why she was always the one with the most smarts. She and Cookie usually had the same ideas but Brianna was the one to execute them.

Ready for the night's events Brianna was dressed very differently than normal and slipped the deejay a note to introduce her as "HONEY". She put on a golden brown wig that looked like something Nicki Minaj would wear with black tips. She wore a gold bikini bathing suit and black patent leather thigh high stiletto boots. Yeah, she was ready to take control of the dance floor tonight and make the money she knew she was capable of.

"Coming to the stage with a new name, new swag and new sex appeal- as if she can get any tastier........ "HONEY"!!!!!!!!!!!"

The sounds of *Make It Rain* by Travis Porter blared through the speakers at maximum speed and Brianna, aka Honey, stepped onto the stage. She owned her new persona and danced on the pole with a multitude of new moves that was guaranteed to bring her the money that she needed for the night to secure an apartment she was eyeing for the next month.

Brianna wound her waist, did splits and seductively made love to the pole before moving down to the lower level where the men were awaiting with 50 and hundred dollar bills. She knew she had to step her game up in order to snag one of them for VIP later. As soon as the thought entered her mind, she was approached with her next client.

"Come 'ere, sweetie. I want you for the night," one man said. His breath smelled like Doublemint gum and he smelled like Chrome cologne. He was actually pretty handsome and his chocolate skin glistened in the strobe lights that lit up the club.

"How much am I worth to you tonight? I mean you want me privately? It's gonna cost you because what I do for you, won't be done for anyone else" Brianna said setting up the evenings bonus.

"I want whatever you can offer me for $2,000!" the stranger whispered in her ear. His hot breath hit her face and she smelled his breath once more causing it to make her moist with excitement. She was ready to do whatever for that type of money. Over in the corner, Cookie was lurking getting her dance on with a regular and she caught Brianna's eye. The plan was set in motion and she finished up her dance and made her way to the VIP.

Brianna led her client into the room and behind the curtains and began to kiss him slowly on the couch. She straddled him and allowed him to touch her all over caressing her ass and hips and breasts. "Mmmmmm, you feel so good, boo," he said.

"I know I do, babe! But don't talk. I want to give you your money's worth." Brianna began to kiss him slowly and slowly climbed off his lap and between his legs to pull his dick out of his pants. He was so aroused that his dick could cut rocks and make diamonds. His eyes rolled in the back of his head and he set his head back to enjoy the moment. At that moment, Cookie came in and stood behind him and removed her top. She placed her breast in his mouth and he began sucking like a child nursing his mother for nourishment.

Cookie removed her purple halter top and began to kiss the gentleman furiously and then walked around to where Brianna was. They were about to make it all worthwhile. Brianna stopped giving him head and sat on the floor while Cookie sat in front of her. All of a sudden, they began kissing like long lost lovers. The gentleman's mouth gaped open at such a sight. He was experiencing his own live porn movie and didn't want to look away for fear of missing something.

Brianna grabbed Cookie and laid her down on the floor so he could see what she was going to do. She began kissing Cookie's thighs, ankles and made her way up between her legs. Cookie barely wore anything but a thong anyway so she just pulled it to the side and began to kiss, lick and suck her slit.

She placed her finger inside of her slit and finger-fucked her while nibbling gently on her clit which was red and protruded through her swollen lips. Cookie moaned in pleasure and looked over while grabbing her breasts to tweak her own nipples. She viewed the gentleman enjoying the view immensely. So much so that he began to jerk his dick to the visual of Brianna between Cookie's legs.

Slowly and gently, Brianna nibbled on Cookie until she broke into a cold sweat and felt herself about to achieve orgasm.

"I'm 'bout to cum, Honey! Oh, my goodness, you gon' make me squirt," Cookie exclaimed and Brianna was ready for it. She removed her face and began to fingerfuck Cookie's pussy until she began to squirt all over. She positioned herself directly into the flow and allowed it to splash all over her face and breasts. She rubbed it into her skin and licked it off of her finger.

"Oh shit!" he exclaimed, and harder and harder began to masturbate to what he just saw. His dick jerked faster and began to drip from arousal. Ready to finish him off and give him what he paid for, Cookie and Brianna began to suck his dick with one at the tip and one at the base playing with his balls. The double stimulation proved too much for him and Brianna felt him throbbing as he was about to ejaculate.

"Get up! Both of you! I'm 'bout to cum!" He said, as he positioned himself in front of both of their faces and blew his thick, creamy wad all over their faces. They both turned to each other and kissed, while playing with it in their mouths and swallowed. This was definitely worth the money they were about to make. He collapsed on the couch and they began to clean up, awaiting their payment for a job well done.

Bittersweet

Money Hungry

The three of them cleaned up with baby wipes and hot towels brought to them by Bear and sat around in a circle, discussing pleasantries and what just happened.

"So, um, you guys know each other pretty well?" the gentleman asked. Brianna gave him a slick smile and Cookie continued to clean up and replaced her halter top.

"Yeah, we know each other pretty well. How 'bout you render payment for services provided and you can know more about us? You didn't care about knowing 'bout us or our names when we had your dick in our mouths." Brianna knew she had him then and punctuated her comment with a smirk.

"Yeah, we are cool. Me and Honey are close. So what's ya name? I've seen you in the spot before but I never knew you were interested in a private party," Cookie said, while she crossed her legs on the floor Indian style. She placed a stick of gum in her mouth and watched Brianna walk over to the front of VIP and hand Bear some money. She was unsure what that was about, but paid it no mind seeing as though what she was about to get would pay her rent for the month and allow her to buy some new clothes for her daughter.

"My name is Greg, and I come to the club quite frequently when I am in town. I'm traveling from Baltimore, Maryland and I usually bring my clients here to wind down. Tonight, my client decided to leave early and I wanted to relax after a long night and I'm glad I did. You ladies were phenomenal!"

Brianna walked back over to Greg and looked him up and down.

"Flattery will get you nowhere, but the money you owe us will get you everywhere!" Brianna said, as she straddled Greg and held out her hand.

"Oh, is that it? You need to be paid? No problem," he said as he moved her off of his lap and counted out 20 one hundred dollar bills. Cookie jumped up and Brianna shot her a look that said *"bitch, don't fuck it up for us"*.

"Thank you for allowing us to service you and your erotic needs," Brianna said with a smile. He counted out another 500 and gave it to Cookie. They really lucked out tonight and both of them racked up $2500!

"I'm sure I'll be back and I thank you for helping me relieve my tension," Greg replied, replacing his coat and exiting the VIP room.

"Why the fuck you jump up like that? You ain't neva seen money before?" Brianna was annoyed at Cookie because she didn't want to make it seem as if she was an amateur when in fact, she had no idea what she was beginning to create. She was on the verge of making changes..... BIG changes and they would begin as soon as possible.

"I've seen money, Brianna. I just got a little excited and didn't want him to change his mind about it, that's all. How much money did we make by the way?" Cookie was already mentally calculating what the evening's little erotic sexcapade was worth.

"For the last 45 minutes, we made over $1200 each!" Brianna exclaimed as she got the money together and placed half in Cookie's hand.

"Damn! This shit is going to help me out this week for real. I needed to pay my rent and pay my babysitter."Brianna was happy to help Cookie out and asked her if she was interested in rocking permanently.

"Would you like to make this money regularly? This can be our side hustle and no one would know a thing. The only person that knows anything is Bear and that's because he's on watch while the room is occupied. I hit him off with extra cash to do it, but I know once our rates go up, we will have to give him a little more."

"Okay, well, I know it's Bear and he's making sure that we are okay and no one attacks us or anything. That's the good thing. You didn't tell anyone else, did you? I don't want Slim to find out and then we get in trouble for extra services."Cookie began to get paranoid and it was irritating Brianna. There was no time or energy to be spent on second guessing her. This plan would have to work in the short time she planned for it in her head to make enough money to bolt.

"You really don't have to do it if you don't want to. I can be the only bitch collecting for extra treats and you will just be out there dancing and being basic for dollars. Do you not see what we made tonight? We made in less than an hour what some basic bitches make for the week. You've got to be excited about that. I asked you to be down. The least you can be is grateful and not fuck it up for me. Your call! I'm doing this again in a few days once I scope out the right target. If you play by my rules, you won't have to want for anything! I'll call you tomorrow."

Brianna walked out of the VIP room, leaving Cookie to clean up the rest of the room and slipped Bear an extra bill. She needed to be sure he wasn't going to snitch to Slim anything that was taking place for fear that could ruin their extra cash. He would surely want to get a piece of the pie and take more than a chunk, ruining chances and claiming it all for himself. She'd have to find a way to make sure he wasn't involved at all and remained clueless of the going's on.

The next day, Brianna went about her usual routine and got something to eat from the Jamaican spot and took it home to eat it. She was excited about all the money that she brought home and also the moves she was making she had almost twenty four hundred dollars saved up and wanted to double that in six months. She was sure the way things were falling into place that it would occur sooner than she expected and also surpassing her expectations.

"Hi, Momma!" Brianna said walking into the house. Fifi was asleep in the couch in the living room and she had clearly been drinking her usual poison of choice Hennessy Black and smoking weed again. For once, there was peace and quiet in the house. Brianna entered her bedroom, threw down her belongings and grabbed her towel to take a shower.

Brianna looked at her figure in the mirror and wondered if her father had any of her features. She always knew her daddy was Spanish, but never knew anything else. When she was a little girl, she would look at all the men walking in and out of the house and wonder if he was her father.

Fifi made it clear to her that they were simply "Uncles" and not to get too comfortable because they wouldn't be around long. That caused Brianna to not give a damn about anyone and she never believed she would fall in love and get married. She loved money more anyway and once money was gone, you got some more. It was harder to get another man that quickly anyway she reasoned.

Brianna finished with the bathroom and went back into her bedroom. She was exhausted and decided she wasn't going to her nursing position and wanted to rest. She had been working nonstop at both jobs and needed a break. She wasn't calling out for work at the Golden Palace. After the money she made the night before she was excited and just needed rest to continue to make extra money off of the customers that were willing to pay.

She fell asleep dreaming of the money that would be coming her way on a regular and nightly basis. She felt hot breath on her skin and it caused her to get hot and uncomfortable. She felt hands touch her in places that she never thought she'd feel after all the clients rarely touched her. She always did things to them or to Cookie.

The dream she was having felt a little too real and Brianna opened her eyes to see Herbie hovering over her with his dick in his hand about to place it in her face.

"What the fuck do you intend on doing with that?" Brianna whispered maliciously. If he had come any closer, she would have been forced to scream and wake up Fifi. She didn't want to do that and ruin the peace in the house for the day. She knew it was too good to be true.

"You didn't think that giving me money was the only thing I'd want from you, did you? I want what everyone else is getting and I want it to be worth my while," Herbie snarled. He had been drinking and smoking with Brianna's mother and was clearly aroused at the vision of Brianna sleeping in her bed.

"The money I gave you is for you to leave me alone period. Why can't you just be satisfied?" Brianna rolled her eyes and tried to get up but Herbie held a grip on her throat that caused her to gasp for air and struggle to swallow.

"NO! It will never be enough. You are always in my way and your fucking mother is useless. The only reason I keep her around is because I get to look at your sexy lil' ass. Now you WILL service me just like I need to be or else I will make sure you are out on your ass sooner than you are planning." Herbie hissed out words that told Brianna that he was serious with his threats and would make good on them. He still had his hand around her throat and she had tears running down her face. She didn't know if it was anger or fear.

"Just tell me what you want me to do and I will do it. I have no more money from you until next week. What do you want instead?" Brianna whispered through gulps not knowing what the answer would be but ready to give him whatever was necessary.

"You know what I want, Brianna. I want you!"

Herbie removed his hand from her neck and slowly ran his hand down her waist to her thigh. She wasn't one to sleep with underwear and he caught her at a fine time. She was so tired and not planning to go to work that night and wanted to relax. She lay down on her bed with just her t-shirt and this mothafukka has caught her with no panties on. Talk about "easy access". Herbie's rough hands grazed her thighs and began to ease between them. Brianna muffled under her breath, scared of what damage would be done, but she already knew what was coming. She was going to be invaded one way or the other.

Her legs were parted and his dirty hands made his way between her legs and eased up to her pussy lips. She fought the feeling of arousal and her pussy tightened up under his touch. She felt his fingers one by one enter her and he began to fingerfuck her slowly. In and out he placed his fingers and took one finger out slowly licking her sweet juices off of it not taking an eye off of her.

"You like that, bitch? You want the dick, don't you? Are you afraid of me?" Herbie asked Brianna, looking at her face filled with tears and trying to mask the pain she felt. He wasn't hurting her physically but the emotional damage that she knew would only continue was something she wasn't prepared to deal with.

"No, I'm not afraid of you but I do want you to leave me alone," she said barely above a whisper. Her eyes were red and she felt her pussy dry up and began to burn due to the penetration of his fingers in her private spot. Brianna wiggled away from his grasp and he didn't fight to regain control. Herbie stood up over Brianna's bed as she cowered and covered herself in a corner on the edge of her bed and pulled out his dick. He had a nice size for an old guy. It was circumcised and curved to the left. A grin grew slowly on his face and she knew exactly what she was about to see.

"What the fuck are you doing," Brianna hissed at Herbie and began to get angry at what she was observing. He jerked his dick back and forth and constantly sniffed his finger that was scented with her pussy juice.

"The next best thing to fucking you!"

Herbie jerked and stroked his dick harder and harder until he began to grunt and moan under his breath. Faster and faster, he pulled his meat stick until it began to throb under pressure. Drips of cum began to leak from the tip and fell onto the bed and he began to tremble and shake faster and faster. Suddenly, after about 10 minutes of constant stimulation, he exploded his seed unto the bed leaving a hot, creamy, sticky mess.

"Ahhhhhhh," Herbie said, at the height of climax, still looking at Brianna. She began to cry hysterically and covered her mouth in her pillow to muffle the sounds. She couldn't believe he actually did that and on her bed, no less.

"I'll be back to get some more. You sure do taste good! How much is that pussy worth now? I get the friends and family discount, I'm sure." Herbie cleaned himself up and slowly walked out of the hallway to go have himself a drink. Brianna got up and closed the door behind him looking out to see if anyone observed what she just did.

She sighed a breath of relief, believing that her mother was asleep in the living room and had no idea what was going on. Sadly, she was mistaken when out of the shadows emerged Fifi with a cigarette in her hand. She had heard and saw everything through a crack in Brianna's door. Everything wasn't as it seemed but sometimes it really doesn't matter once the idea has been produced. Nothing will ever be the same again; as if it ever was to begin with.

Biting off More Than One Can Chew

A few days had passed since the incident with Herbie and she had been working extra hard in order to avoid him, but still provided him with the hush money needed to continue living comfortably. She and Cookie racked up no less than $1500 every night and they loved the extra money. Slim still had no clue and Bear was comfortable getting hit off with an extra 100 to 250 dollars extra a night.

One particular night, Cookie caught Brianna before work with an idea of her own and while she felt she was going to be able to go through with it, it would most certainly set into motion the end of their friendship as they knew it.

Just as Brianna got to work and was in the locker room putting on her costume for the night, Cookie came up to her nervously.

"What's up, bitch," Cookie said, sheepishly, trying to break the ice. She knew that Brianna wasn't in the best of moods lately but she wanted to show her alliance with her was still strong.

"Hey, Cookie! What's up with you today? You ready for tonight? I was thinking this time you could do me for a change. They always see you be the receiver so this time I'd allow you to take charge and I can lay there and you can do whatever you think will make us this money tonight."

Cookie was taken aback by this approach by Brianna and decided she would wait to propose them separating their act and claiming money on their own.

"Yeah, that fine. Whatever it takes to get this money, right? You okay? You seem kind of off lately." Cookie was observing Brianna's behavior but didn't ask too many questions. She was being obedient especially after the last time Brianna spazzed out on her. She would never ask her for fear of rejection but she liked Brianna more than she was willing to admit to anyone and always wanted to look out for her and make her happy.

"I'm good. Just a lot on my mind and I've been working more hours to stay busy. What time are we on with our set because I'm not coming out the locker room until time. I need to rest up a little bit because I'm a little stressed." Brianna was about to rest her head and relax when her cell phone rang. She was surprised to see the name on it since it had been weeks since they spoke.

"Hello?" Brianna said while a slow smile crept across her face. She needed this distraction and this one was worth it. Cookie looked on while the conversation continued and Brianna looked at her with a hint of attitude wondering if she would take the cue that she was now busy and couldn't entertain her.

"Cookie, can you excuse me please while I take this call. You and I will talk before I come out in a little while ok?"

Brianna waited patiently for Cookie to get the hint and she gave her a weird look as if she wanted to know what was so important that she couldn't talk in front of her.

"A'ight, Bri, no problem. You and I will talk in a little while." Cookie said while walking out. She took one look back and shook her head. She was tired of being the follower in the friendship and decided that it was time to be the lead dog instead of always looking at Brianna's ass in the front of the line.

"Hey, ma! I was waiting for you to call but I guess you weren't that type of woman. I wanted to know if we could link up for dinner this evening." It was Antoine and he hadn't spoken to Brianna in a while, but the connection that they shared was unmistakable.

"Ummm tonight ? What time? I am at work and I won't be getting off anytime soon." Brianna was getting worried that he would find out her secret as a stripper and ruin what could possibly be the beginning of a beautiful relationship. She didn't want for it to be over before it even began.

"Well, I have some business I need to handle but I can pick you up from work and we can..." Brianna immediately interrupted his next thought and broke out into a cold sweat upon thinking that she would see him.

"No, you don't have to pick me up from work. I can go home and meet you at home and then we can go from there."

Brianna thought quickly on her feet, wanting to hide that part of her life from him. She wanted to leave a good impression but knew that sooner than later that part would come out sooner than she expected. She would let him know and he could do what he wanted with the information but for now her life would remain private.

"Nah, I'm going to be running around so you can call me and we can take it from there. I don't want to make you uncomfortable." Antoine ended the call and scratched his head but then chuckled. He was too concerned about getting money to be chasing pussy. He liked the chase of the almighty dollar and that was constant and never deceived him.

Bitches usually bolted on him when they've had enough of him. He couldn't take his chances getting attached to someone that wouldn't always be there for him. Money never failed him he felt but all that was going to change.

Antoine's phone rang and he answered it. He was hoping it was Brianna but no such luck. His heart had betrayed him unbeknownst to him and he was feeling her more than he would consciously admit to.

"Yo!" He said, answering the phone.

"My nig, you got some people in Soundview lookin' to get some perks! Can you come through real quick? Homie wants it to be real discreet because he's a city worker and can't afford to get jammed up." The caller was one of Antoine's workers and kept it short and sweet.

"Say no more! I'm on it in 20 minutes!"

No sooner had the phone rang had Antoine been in the car on the way to Hunts Point Avenue in the Bronx. He had a bag of

Perks and was ready to collect some cash for a previous transaction. He pulled up to Hunts Point and picked up his homeboy "Tiny".

Tiny wasn't really small with his 6'7" stature. He traveled with Antoine when there was a transaction that took place just in case niggas wanted to act up and not pay. He was also well aware and always looked out when Antoine needed him for backup. He's been there much like a brother and has been his right hand when no one else was there. He shared his love of money and was paid handsomely for his services.

"A'ight, so what we gotta do?" Tiny said to Antoine always ready for action just in case he must watch Antoine's back. People call him a bodyguard but he prefers to called his henchmen or right hand

"Easy, killa! I'ma just drive on over to the spot and drop off the goods. I know exactly who you spoke to. No worries my man. He's cool wit me." Antoine reached over and turned on the radio to Hot 97 and just in time for one of his favorite songs by rapper Drake.

The song made him speed up on the Bruckner Expressway and within a few minutes he was right where he needed to be. What he didn't know was he was right where Brianna was a few days ago.

The men entered the building like old friends but not before securing their weapons behind their back. They couldn't take for granted that this deal could go wrong. Their lives were always at stake even though they took pride in being careful.

"Can I say who you'd like to see?" the security guard motioned for them to come by and sign their names on the visitors list and asked them to step aside.

"Yeah, I wanna see my uncle, Herbie. He works here and I gotta get some money for my mom," Antoine said, since he looked the youngest and most innocent.

"Oh okay, well let me notify him that his nephews are here for him." The guard called Herman downstairs and he walked over to them giving the guard the side eye.

"What's up, Uncle Herb?" Antoine said, watching to see if there was any tension. He could always tell if there was a vibe and how the sale would go by watching the movements of the person he was with.

"Hey, Tony. Your aunt has something for me I heard. Let me go grab my stuff and we can go hang out like the good old days."Herbie turned around and went back upstairs to retrieve his bag. He was ready to go anyway and this gave him a reason to drink, smoke and be merry.

Herbie returned and the three men walked out towards the car and it was all smiles. They made the exchange and decided it was late enough to go get something to eat. Antoine never mixed business with pleasure, but he wanted to let Herbie know that he would no longer be supplying him with the weed and Perk that he desired. He had his mind set on a bigger profit and this one would bring in more revenue and less exposure.

The men entered TGIFridays and ordered drinks at the bar before they proceeded to sit down and discuss the plans to end their operation. Herbie ordered a Bud Light and the other two men decided on Guinness.

"So, what's the plan now?" Herbie inquired because he wanted to be sure that although he was satisfied with Perk and weed he could use them as an option just in case he wanted to go a little bit stronger. He wasn't sure

83

what else they were going to do but just in case it was always good to seek out a replacement.

Antoine took a sip of the Guinness and placed it on the bar table. As soon as he was about to speak, the waitress stepped up to place their order. They were informed they needed to order food in order to remain there. They ordered mozzarella sticks, hot wings and nachos. Something was better than nothing and that was exactly how they all felt about the current situation regarding their money and product.

"I want to make a clean break of this. I've got other things brewing and I've been stashing dough to make a connect in Maryland. If you want to stay on board, then you'll be required to pay double but you will get almost half of what you are already supplied with." Antoine had already thought this over in his head and was satisfied with his projected revenue even though it hadn't come to fruition.

Herbie sat back and ate the appetizers and thought about how he himself could flip the outcome of his own profit. He never let Fifi take all the pills. He handled his own business on the side with the fellas at the job. Only a few choice individuals were allowed to join him on his binges but mostly he did it with Fifi as they kept her under control. She was at times a volatile creature but she for the most part was sexy as hell. Herbie liked to keep her around for that reason. He loved to see her submissive and sexy.

He thought back to a week ago when he came home from work. Herbie knew he left her a dosage to take and her usual bottle of Vodka and she knew to take them about eleven o'clock in the morning so when he came home she would be good and ready to do the kinky shit he liked.

"Herbie, baby! Whatchu doin' over there? Come'ere and suck my titties," Fifi said, as she stood up on the bed in red fishnet stockings and a black see-through teddy. She was good and ready to be fucked by him that afternoon because she was bored and horny. She also wanted to give him something else to think about aside from Brianna. Fifi knew about his obsession with her, but she let it slide because she knew nothing was going to come from it.

"Woman, you know what I like! Lay down so I can feast," Herbie said, as he dropped his duffle bag on the floor. He still had on his Timberland boots and his shirt on and walked over to the bed. He eyeballed the satin sashes she had near the bedside table and conjured up in his head a way to relieve himself from a hard day's work. He was going to punish Fifi in a way she will never forget.

They always played kinky love games and she never remembered them until later on after she woke up from her liquor and drug induced binge. This time she would possibly remember it more so than any other time. Herbie was a little annoyed that particular day because he lost two customers after not having enough Perk to resell to them at work. No Perk meant no money, which meant he was out $1500 that could have gone toward more drugs and liquor to keep Fifi quiet. Her social security was going to run out without him being able to take that trip to Miami and meeting up with a connect named Jose.

"Bend over with your ass up!" Fifi did as she was told and lift up her nightgown waiting with glazed eyes for what Herbie was about to do. Fifi was the most submissive when she consumed some liquor and this time was no different.

"Aye, chulo, come gimme what I been waiting for all day," Fifi said, exhibiting her Spanglish skills to Herbie. Her desire was becoming more and more apparent and she loved how he did whatever he wanted to her. She wanted a man to boss her around and take charge and he did. Fifi felt her pussy throb with anticipation as she felt her hands being tied to the rungs of the bed board. She was being restrained with the red sash and also blindfolded so when she was to receive her punishment for being a bad girl was to be a sweet surprise.

Herbie loved when Fifi listened and stood up in his boxers and wife beater still wearing his Timberland boots. He wet his finger and placed it around the rim of Fifi's asshole making it wet and twitch. He stuck his face between her cheeks and began to lick, suck and tongue-fuck her asshole preparing it for the erotic torture it was about to endure. He licked her ass hole until she shivered and she placed her concealed face into the pillow beneath her chin. She bit the pillow and screamed in pleasure. He loved hearing her beg for mercy and rotated his tongue in and out of her anal cavity until she could barely remain on her knees.

He gave her a few minutes to recuperate and was at it again but this time began playing with her pussy at the same time. She climaxed within minutes but couldn't move due to the restraints. All you heard was the sounds of the moaning beneath the scarf that was embedded in her mouth. Ready to punish her sexually, he pulled her ass close to him and entered her asshole with a swift thrust. Fifi was aroused enough for it to not be too painful but it was still stinging because of the surprise due to the blindfolds.

Herbie's dick pummeled in and out of her bottom and grasped his tool tightly and he grunted in erotic pleasure. He played with her clit and she squirted in his hand while bucking under pressure. He wanted to more and more of her and removed his dick from her asshole.

"You didn't take a shit, did you?" he asked her, smelling what were some remnants of shit that coated his dick.

"No, baby! I didn't today." Fifi smiled, not knowing what to expect but being the submissive woman she was right now prepared herself for anything.

"Good! Come suck my dick and make it wet!" Herbie said guiding her to his throbbing dick. Without warning he pushed it in her mouth and she gagged at the taste of shit several times but didn't vomit. She actually got turned on and began to suck harder and harder turning him on more and more. He began yelling at her and grabbed the back of her head throwing his back in orgasmic bliss.

"Suck it, bitch," Herbie said, while fucking her face and playing with her nipples, rapidly tweaking them between his fingers. She obeyed and took it all into his mouth inch by inch until her jaws were packed with his chocolate member. His pre-cum began to ooze from the tip and he literally grew harder and within a few more minutes he would be ready to release.

He wanted to punish her some more so he pushed her down on the bed and pushed his dick deep within her leaking pussy without so much as a word. She was so wet there was a puddle beneath her as she came instantly.

"This is my pussy, bitch! This is my pussy! Tell me this is my pussy!" Herbie said repeatedly but then he realized she couldn't oblige him because of the gag in her mouth and pulled it down off her lips so she could respond to his demands.

"It's your pussy, baby! It's all yours!" Fifi said, gasping between thrusts. She was about to explode and her panting revealed the climb of ecstasy she was experiencing. Him hearing her say that brought about a rush of excitement and after repeating it for a few minutes he couldn't take it anymore and removed his dick from her pussy and placed it in her mouth releasing all of his erupting semen onto her face. All that was heard was gurgling sounds and groans of pleasure.

"Yo, nigga, what the fuck you thinking 'bout over there?" Antoine abruptly shaking him from his erotic trip down memory lane. He didn't like to feel ignored and took a swig of beer waiting for Herbie to respond to him.

"Yo, my man, I'm sorry. I was just thinking 'bout some good ass pussy I had the other night." Herbie grinned and laughed because he was thinking about Brianna when he was fucking Fifi. That's something that makes him cum harder than ever and he said if he ever gets the chance to do that he was going to make it very memorable. If he was able to fuck both mother and daughter that would be a nigga's dream come true.

"Yeah well, it's not 'bout pussy! Its 'bout that cash and I don't give a fuck who you are thinking about. I need my money to be stable in hand and no one needs to fuck with it or else they'll be problems."

Antoine was focused on getting the money that was needed to execute this deal in Miami. He was tired of making small moves in NY and wanted to take it to the South. He already secured two connects-one in Miami and was working on one in ATL. The plans were in motion but people were getting in his way and he was tired of picking up the slack.

"Yo, I need to relax after a hard day's work. Are you done here? Because I have more things to ponder before I make these power moves. Any suggestions?" Antoine looked to the men for ideas on recreation and Bear responded.

"How 'bout the Golden Palace? I heard the bitches in there have the fattest asses."

"The, the Golden Palace?" Herbie stuttered and stammered upon hearing Brianna's place of business mentioned.

"There something wrong with that spot. son?" Antoine looked at Herbie's face and he noticed how uncomfortable he was at the mention of a local spot that had no significance to him.

"Oh, no, well, you know I got wifey at home and she might feel a way if I go to a titty bar, but I'm down. This is business though and we need to chill after so she doesn't need to know. Let's roll!"

The men left the restaurant and ventured to The Golden Palace, not knowing what to expect but what Herbie didn't know was that this was going to be an extra interesting evening and one he would never forget.

Bittersweet

Revelations

Cookie sat in the dressing room and looked at the clock. It was almost time for Brianna to come in and she was going to be pleased with the turnout. There was a new DJ coming to showcase some new music and whenever that happened it prompted a lot of new faces in the crowd. This DJ was one of the less popular but still relevant ones from the local radio station and he was focused on building up his catalogue. What a lot of the dancers knew was that when a DJ came through they usually picked the hottest dancer to give their best music to as an entrance theme.

Cookie and Brianna were both vying for that top stop although they worked together in the VIP section that's something they didn't depend on. Any given night they can make one to one thousand dollars each but being the top dancer can net them each two thousand dollars easily.

Cookie lived in the Bronx near Third Avenue and didn't work any other job but this one. She needed to make a certain amount of money to take care of her three year old daughter because she lived on her own with her own bills. This job was really her livelihood and she needed every dime to make her life a little content. When Brianna got the idea for the special VIP, she was skeptical because she didn't know what it would entail but the more and more she got into it she felt that this wasn't prostitution and she was just providing an extra service to those that paid to see her dance exotically anyway.

Looking in the mirror and seeing the scar on her left cheek she reflected on life and how far she'd come and how much more she'd need to go before that thing called "happiness" entered her very complicated life. Her face reflected that of a miserable woman but certainly the men didn't regard her as ugly because they still loved to see her dance.

Her chocolate brown skin resembled milk chocolate cocoa and her hair looked like the Indian Remy sold on 125th Street in Harlem that everyone desired. Hers wasn't a lace front and she wore it long much like Pocahontas with a part in the middle. Her breasts were small B cups but she was satisfied because the men loved her tiny waist and her fat ass that stuck out like a shelf. She had the ability to make it clap and dance at will exciting the men that viewed it every night.

No matter how she looked, though, she always felt like she was less than beautiful because of her scar which she earned from her ex-boyfriend's girlfriend. She jumped her in a dark alley and sliced her face after discovering that the relationship between her and her ex didn't end. The woman had no mercy and while they were fighting spit razor blades that were hidden in the side of her sneakers.

The razor blades dug into her face slicing into her left cheek causing wounds that would give her the complex she has now. The one that was the most prominent caused Cookie to receive seventeen stitches and almost lose an eye if it was any closer.

She never forgave her ex-boyfriend who was her child's father and decidedly moved out of Brooklyn into the Bronx beginning a new life with her child. He's attempted contact but with no success because she's refused to see him out of fear for her child's life. His wife's day was coming soon but it was the baby that mattered most.

Every day that she looks in the mirror, she remembers what kind of sacrifice love is and vowed never to love anyone again for fear of getting hurt. The emotional scars last much longer than the physical badge she sports daily!

"Bitch, are you listening to me? DJ Grime is out there and he's already packing the house!" Brianna interrupted Cookie's thoughts with her excitement. She dropped her duffle bag on the bag and took a look at Cookie.

"What the hell got your mood sour? You better liven that shit up because there's a whole lotta money out there to be made and I've got bills to pay" Brianna needed to make about five thousand dollars to pay for school, pay off Herbie and to save the rest of the money to move. She was determined to get out of the house with her mom and Herbie but the more she saved, the more something came up to snatch whatever money she had for other purposes.

"I've just been here thinking about life and what I need to do. I was also thinking of a way to get the VIP to come to us. Let's take some of our act onto the stage. I mean we are the top bitches in the club right now so it only makes sense that they know who we are and why niggas are spending their money for us. It's sure to help get us the most cash tonight". Cookie was behind on her rent a month and a half due to her hidden extravagant spending habits. She also drank like a fish but her affinity for the latest bags and shoes made it hard for her. She liked to "pay herself first" and spent a lot of money on clothes for work as well as her daughter.

"Well, snap the fuck out of it!" Brianna said, perusing her locker and pulled out a hot red jumpsuit with sequins and cutouts. She paraded around the locker room stripping instantly stepping out of her clothes. Brianna knew of the advantage it would be to make the most money on a night where there were ballers in the house. She actually thought over Cookie's suggestion and was going to respond when she saw Cookie eyeballing her lustfully.

"You see something you like?" Brianna stuck her finger in her exposed pussy and wiped her juices on her thong which was in her other hand. She walked over to Cookie and waved it under her nose.

"I see the way you look at me. Remember, its business and I don't like pussy all the time. I like you, though, and if you really wanna get a taste, maybe after I stack my chips and move you can help me christen my new place." Brianna blew a kiss at Cookie who in turn reached out to get more but was met with air.

Her feelings for Brianna were growing more intense and she thought of her more than a coworker. This was something she didn't think would happen but lately they became more and more and the urge was becoming uncontrollable.

Cookie thought about how she would perform tonight without showing way too much attraction and keeping it business, but after smelling Brianna, her mood changed and all she wanted was a taste. She walked over to her locker and picked out a black crotch-less number with studs and cut outs on the nipples. She got some silver tassels to cover them up during the show. She got ready in the corner and with confidence knew that tonight would be a night everyone would remember forever.

A few hours had passed and it was almost time for the girls to get on stage. The deejay had introduced them and Cookie and Brianna looked at each other in anticipation. Tonight would be the night where they would possibly become the head dancers on the stage. This wasn't just a performance in front of some of the music industry's hottest stars; it was also an audition of sorts and the highlight of their dancing career.

Brianna got on the stage first and began to work the pole grinding and humping and fucking it as if it was a man with a dick. She climbed up to the top and did a remarkable split and within minutes, Cookie came out taking over the bottom of the pole. The way she laid, when Brianna slid down the pole their legs were on opposite sides of the pole and in a "scissors" position. Their pussies were only separated by the pole and they reached over and grabbed the other's breasts.

Cookie pinched Brianna's nipples and she tweaked it making her moan in excitement. For once, Cookie was commandeering the dominant position in the performance and, while Brianna had wanted this before, she wasn't sure she wanted it tonight. If she didn't stand up and take her position back Cookie would be the spotlighted dancer and she couldn't risk that with all that she needed to accomplish. Cookie leaned in for a kiss and Brianna hissed at her under her breath.

"Don't think you're gonna fuck it up for me. I'll steal your shine before you even begin to glimmer!" Cookie looked at her as her eyes squinted in disapproval. She knew what she was doing was working but not to the extent to which she planned. Cookie was just doing what Brianna wanted done. Clearly, sometimes you can't give people what they want and with that thought crossing her mind, she went to the extreme to show them that she was the choice they wanted for the featured performances. After all, the more money she made, the less she had to worry about depending on Brianna's trifling ass.

Cookie eased over and kissed Brianna biting her bottom lip gently in the process. She came from around the pole and stood up dancing around Brianna and placing her right leg on her shoulder. Brianna grabbed her ankle and began kissing it gently, allowing her tongue to graze the boniest area, giving Cookie shivers. Even though she felt shown up, she refused to crumble under the pressure. This just made her step her game up even more.

Brianna laid Cookie on the ground and began to dance seductively on top of her grinding her as if they were having dry sex. The crowd began to quiet down and watch the performance with awe and excitement. Men began to dig into their wallets and toss dollar bills on the stage gently hitting the women in their ass and on their thighs.

The glass stilettos they wore stepped on the crumpled money while they continued to dance about the stage. Cookie knew that Brianna was attempting to remain dominant and she wasn't having it. Brianna wore a crotch-less number and it was easy access for what Cookie was about to do. She flipped Brianna over and began to finger fuck her pussy hard to the rhythm of the music playing. The DJ made sure that it was something seductive, yet upbeat.

"What the fuck are you doing?" Brianna hissed while gasping to regain composure. Cookie had her right where she wanted and Brianna loved the feeling although her body was betraying her mind. Cookie removed her finger, rubbed it on Brianna's lips and then bent down to kiss her sensually. Tasting Brianna's nectar on her lips made her pussy wet and they both became moist wanting to do so much more, but without an audience.

"I am taking control of my destiny. If you want it, cum get it!" Cookie said, knowing she had the upper hand. She wasn't letting Brianna take her shine but was going to give her a chance to battle for it. Cookie took Brianna's left leg and placed it on her right shoulder leaving the audience to see her lick, suck, nibble and bite her swollen and over stimulated clit. Brianna moaned on the stage and removed her top allowing her breasts to billow over the top revealing her erect nipples.

"Aye, save some of that shit for me. I wanna join in!" a noisy patron said, as he saw Brianna writhing on the floor in ecstasy. Even the DJ abandoned the booth briefly to see what was really going on and what was causing most of the men to have erections. The girl on girl action was turning all of them on and they didn't know what to do with themselves. They wanted to stop looking but it was a seductive train wreck that they didn't want to remove their eyes from. The next best thing was to pay them for their services and if all went well they would get their chances at a few VIPs that night.

"Yo, son, check out the dudes at the stage," Tiny said as he, Antoine and Herman walked into the Golden Palace on one of its busiest nights. The place was packed wall to wall with men listening to music and receiving lap dances from the women that were on the floor. The most popular spot was the main stage where Cookie and Brianna were performing.

"That's the hot spot for sure and I'm gonna make sure I get VIP status," Antoine said, as he began to make his way to through the crowd. Brianna began to moan loudly while Cookie continued to lingually punish her oozing slit. She didn't realize two men that played important roles in her life were present. Her head was thrown back in bliss, oblivious anyone else or her surroundings.

"Oooooh, eat that pussy! Damn girl, I can come join you if you need help!" Antoine said, as he watched Cookie. Brianna' hair covered her face and she moved her head from side to side as she approached orgasm. Cookie was about to make her cum and this orgasm would be like nothing she'd experienced being with a woman.

Cookie continued to punish Brianna's pussy and began to squeeze her clit with her lips while fingering her tight hole. Both stimulants created pressure and Brianna couldn't hold it in anymore. She began to cum right there on that stage. Her pussy contracting and releasing fluids on Cookie's hand and face causing everyone in the audience to gasp in amazement.

Few of the men there had ever seen or encountered a squirter, and this was something that they would mark down in their mental diaries. Many of them grabbed their crotch to tame their erections that were poking through their jeans at rapid paces.

"Oh, MY GOD!" Brianna screamed, yelped and convulsed on the stage causing her to feel disoriented. She hadn't noticed Antoine or Herbie in the audience until it was too late.

"Brianna?" Antoine recognized Brianna instantly. His eyes confirmed what his heart had been battling. He was feeling her and couldn't believe that the woman he wanted to be his was a stripper.

"Yo, you see this shit, Herb? This bitch is a stripper. I was gonna wife her ass, too, but now I can't even be too sure." Antoine was trying to process everything but it was coming too fast. Herbie's face contained a smirked look of satisfaction knowing that he didn't have to do a thing to potentially ruin Brianna's life. She did it all on her own and he didn't need to lift a finger.

"Antoine? Oh shit!" Brianna ran off the stage and left Cookie to pick up all the money that was thrown at them. She also noticed Herbie in the audience and was convinced that he brought Antoine to the spot and for that betrayal; he cemented her demise in stone. She was ready to make his life even more of a living hell than she was already working on.

They made easily $2000 during that short performance, but Cookie was happy to know that she was the star of the show this time and Brianna was easily outshined. The cards were held by Cookie and she just played the game and ultimately won.

Bittersweet

Shock to the System

Brianna ran back into the dressing room and began to sob without regards for who heard her. She was losing control of her life and she didn't like it one bit. Her home life was in disarray and her mother's boyfriend and her potential mate just saw her at her night job. Who knows who else has seen her at the Golden Palace and hasn't said anything but is ready to blackmail her. She couldn't take that chance and decided to take a break for a while until she figured things out.

Brianna removed her make-up and clothing and threw on some sweats, gathering her things to leave. She was about to exit through the back door when she saw Cookie standing there counting her money. Just who she needed to see and with rage taking over her body, she decided to confront her about the little stunt she pulled.

"Bitch, are you fucking crazy? That wasn't a part of the plan! You and I save those types of performances for VIP! Do you know how much trouble we could get into?" Brianna began yelling at Cookie wanting to smack her face for not paying attention.

"I just did what I needed to do in order to secure positions. It worked and the DJ just made the both of us headliners at his show. He's going to pay us $3000 to perform like that every time we do what we did tonight."

"You think I give a fuck about what the DJ thinks? My life has been possibly ruined because of your greed! I have been outed by my mother's boyfriend and the dude I was talking to was standing right next to him! I can't come back here for a few days." Brianna began pacing back and forth trying to quickly figure things out.

"Tell everyone I got sick and had to leave and I'll be back in a week. Tell them I had an emergency and have to go out of town. When I come back we'll be better than ever, perform three more times and then we'll have about 10 to 25 grand. After that, I am done. I'm moving away and getting my life in order so I don't have to deal with this bullshit anymore," Brianna said beginning to walk away.

"Where the fuck do think you are going? You aren't going anywhere just yet. You are indebted to me and you leaving isn't such a good idea right now because we have unfinished business. You see, "HONEY", you and I are now a team and you need me to make this money. I need you to fuck me like I need to be fucked and you will comply with this or else I will out you permanently.You didn't think you were just going to walk around here free and clear and I wasn't going to require anything? Bitch, you have lost your damn mind"

Brianna's mouth was gaped open with horror. She had truly created a monster and now she had another enemy to contend with. How did it all go spiraling out of control? She had to form some type of alliance and quick and she knew just who she had to talk to in order to make that happen. For now, she was going to 'play fool to catch wise' as the truth would be revealed.

"No problem, Cookie. I will stay put for now, but I do need a few days. That guy was trying to be my boyfriend and I want to repair things with him." Brianna was thinking of any reason to get the hell out of dodge but without pissing Cookie off any more than she did.

"How much money is for me by the way? They paid you already?" Brianna eyeballed the wad of cash in Cookie's hand and calculated quickly that she had to get at least $8000 to make her goal and move like she wanted to. Everything else was second place as far as she was concerned including her mother.

"I knew that you would come to your senses when you see how much money I was holding on to. This is about three Gs I've got and this is only from the men in the crowd. Here's your portion." Cookie handed her less than half and Brianna knew that she wouldn't be honest but she'd have to settle in order to make her plan succeed. Greed was something that everyone had to deal with in their own way and how you survived after it backfired was your karma

"Thanks, Cookie. Thanks a lot and I'm sure this will come in handy more than you think." She smiled at her, adjusted her bag over her shoulder and walked out. She would be going to use this money to flip it and exact revenge on those who needed a lesson to be taught. It would be a whole new ballgame very soon and she would be on the winning team.

Brianna went home and went to sleep because bright and early she was ready to go to her job as the home health aide. She wasn't going to give that up until she was straight with her money. She walked up the stairs to her brownstone with keys in hand like she normally did but this time it was silent. Brianna rarely walked into the house without being greeted with violence and aggravation. This was a generous surprise yet she wondered what foolishness would meet her on the other side of the door. She put the key in the door and turned it to the side opening it slowly.

"Momma?" she called out to Fifi, who was nowhere to be found. She figured she would be at peace and exhaled a sigh of relief as she made her way towards her bedroom. Her relief turned to sadness when she opened her bedroom door and found her clothes strewn all over the place. From corner to corner, she saw her shoes, costumes from work, money and wigs all around her bedroom. Lying within the midst of it, with a bottle of vodka, was her mother on her bed. She was drunk as a skunk and had been wearing the same clothes from the night before.

Brianna dropped her bag on the floor and rushed over to her mother who upon hearing her voice, began to awaken in a violent fury laced with profanity.

"Fucking whore! Can't trust you for shit! You ain't nothing! I can't believe I have a daughter like you. I wish I had an abortion instead of going shopping. A lot of fucking good you did. The clothes woulda been more reliable than your trifling ass!" slurred Fifi, in her drunken stupor, still holding the bottle and spilling liquor all over the place.

"Momma, why you just can't stay off that shit? Why do you have to treat me like that? And you wonder why I stay out at night and stay working so I don't have to deal with you or Herbie!" Brianna wasn't going to bite her tongue even though she knew that her mom wasn't in her right mind, but they say alcohol is the devil's truth serum and Fifi was telling her exactly how she felt about her whether she wanted to hear it or not. After the night she had, Brianna was also going to speak her own version of the truth and who didn't like it, "Oh well!"

Brianna walked around to her bed and began to place the clothes on the floor when she was met with a crack to the skull by a bottle her mother was holding. Fifi had become a violent drunk and knocked out Brianna, causing blood to spew from her temple.

"Momma, no!" she said, holding her skull which began to bleed from the injury. Never had her mother hit her and this was one of the times when she needed her the most. Fifi realized what she did and began to wake out of her drunken stupor.

"Brianna! Baby! I'm so sorry!" she said, reaching out to her. Brianna crawled back toward the bed while holding her head with a shirt off of the floor. Fifi realized what she had done and began to sober up but it was too late. Brianna had reached her breaking point and she couldn't take it anymore.

With one hand, she grabbed her secret stash, her purse and the money Cookie just gave her and she was out.Everyone wanted to entice the bitch in her to come out and, now that it has arrived, there was NO turning back.

Let's Start A Riot!

Brianna grabbed her head which began to throb in pain. She was confused and disoriented about what to do and where to go, seeing as how everyone she initially thought had her back turned on her. She was all alone in more ways than she used to think. Brianna trekked down the street with her bags and prayed someone would reach out and help her but no such luck. Going back to her mother was off limits for now. Her abusively volatile behavior was too much to handle.

She was still in shock that she hit her and forgiveness wasn't an option. *Damn New Yorkers can be ruthless,* she thought while walking down the street with her head injury. It was a noticeable gash but no one paid her any attention. She was just another casualty of the mean streets. Suddenly help came from a simple phone call and she was shocked to find out who her savior was.

"Hello!" Brianna said as she answered her cell phone and was surprised to hear who was on the other end.

"Yo, Brianna!" Antoine, aka Rico, said and she was embarrassed but felt a sigh of relief to know he still cared a bit. He was driving around the city and decided to give her a call after he left the club. Antoine wasn't one to judge, but he wanted to know why such a beautiful girl like her was stripping in the club.

"Oh, my God! Antoine! I can't tell you how happy I am to hear your voice. I am in such a fucked up place right now and I have no place to go. I am tired and hurt and I only have what I took with me. My life is filled with so much drama!" Brianna said as she broke down on the phone. Antoine heard her sobbing and told her to stay still.

"Honey, stay where you are and I will come get you. Tell me exactly where you are and I will come scoop you and we'll get you cleaned up." Antoine was ready to be the knight in shining armor that Brianna had always wished for, but he was jumping the gun without knowing. See, his heart was betraying him and he didn't even know that he was trying to rescue her no questions asked.

Realistically, she felt like she was a whore perpetrating to be a lady. Antoine didn't feel the same and decided to look past that because he really felt her situation was as fucked up if not more than she was saying. He would soon realize that he was 100% correct. She never judged him for what he did and she surely had an idea. Dealing in illegal activity was common where they lived and he was a bit too young and too 'hood to look like he was a Wall Street banker.

Brianna told him that she was waiting for him in McDonald's on 116th and Lenox Avenue and he made his way to go pick her up and get her safely situated.

"I gotchu mami!" Antoine said on his Bluetooth as he drove through traffic. His partner in crime Tiny came along with him just in case he needed him but only for the ride. Nothing of importance was going to pop off tonight Antoine assured but the extra muscle was always a welcome sight. He never knew when someone would try to roll up on him and with Tiny watching his back it would be difficult for them to succeed.

Brianna sat and wondered why Antoine would want to help her but then shook it off. He must want pussy and she decided that she would fuck him and get it over with. Maybe some head would make him feel better because that's all everyone ever seems to want anyway. Her thoughts were interrupted when she saw him pull up and he helped her into the car. Brianna's head injury wasn't severe but she needed medical attention. Antoine knew someone at Harlem Hospital that was able to get her the help she needed and she was stitched up; and out within thirty minutes.

"So, where you wanna go now, mami?" Antoine said, staring at Brianna with softness in his eyes that surprised even him. She looked so tired that all he wanted to do was take care of her because it seemed all she did was take care of others.

"I don't know. I can give you what money I have for helping me. I appreciate it a lot," she said with tears in her eyes.

"Nah, I ain't takin' shit from you. Let's get you some clothes and you can come chill wit me for the weekend. You've got some painkiller to take so I'll order take out and you can relax, okay?"

"Okay," she said not knowing what else to say because she was used to having to pay her own way regardless. Her phone rang and she saw it was her mother calling her. She pressed ignore and stuck her phone in her pocket.

"Ya man checkin' to see where you are?" Antoine chuckled and asked her sounding jealous without even realizing it. Brianna looked at him and rolled her eyes.

"What the hell is your problem? Yo, I was just joking, but you're 'tuded up so I'm inclined to think that I am right."

"No, that's not my man. I don't have a man. I take care of myself and no nigga does for me. All niggas do is take! That was my mother and she's the reason why I had to go to the fuckin' hospital. She cracked my head with a bottle of vodka while we were arguing. She was drunk, but I am still pissed and can't find it in my heart to forgive her just yet, if at all." Brianna began to sob and Antoine felt like shit for thinking that she was hiding something like another dude from him. He had no right to intrude and wanted to make it up to her.

"Awww, baby, I'm sorry! I didn't mean to upset you. Can I be ya man then?" he said, grinning and kissing her hand. They pulled into Walmart and he gave her $100 to buy whatever she needed for the next few days while she stayed with him. She began to feel so comfortable around him, but didn't want to let him know this. He saw it in her actions, however, when she smiled at him while getting in the car.

They finally arrived in his apartment in Westchester Condominiums and Brianna was amazed at the setup. Everything looked so different on the outside than on the inside. She underestimated him and his ability to make a house a home. He handed her a towel, robe and washcloth and she entered the bathroom to get cleaned up and dressed for bed. He would handle food for the night and ordered Thai from the local restaurant. Antoine rarely cooked and tonight, while he usually ordered something boring and mundane, he wanted to give Brianna a taste of a new world. A world that she could get used to as her and him got closer.

Tiny, his partner left them both alone for the night seeing as how this wasn't business and Antoine requested some time alone. He always liked to meditate and Tiny reminded him of the life he was hoping to leave behind in a few years. He took off his Timbs and grabbed the remote.

The end of the basketball game with the New York Knicks and Chicago Bulls was on and he was interested in catching the last few quarters.

"Hey, Antoine," Brianna said so timidly that Antoine forgot that she was there. She had on some grey sweat pants and a white wife beater that hardly covered her ample bosom. Brianna made her way over to the couch and sat on the other side so as not to disturb him.

"Whatchu doin' all the way over there, mama? I don't want you so far from me ever again," Antoine said tapping the couch next to him.

He motioned for her to come closer and she did just as she asked. He put his arm around her and they watched the game until they both fell asleep on the couch. Brianna awoke with her head in his lap and he was holding her tight. She was scared to move but did so in order to check the bandage on her head. Her hair was in the way and she needed to put it in a ponytail and take meds.

"Where are you going? I told you I didn't want you far from me. You thought I was playing? Tiny ain't here, but I'm gonna be your bodyguard from now on." Antoine got up to follow her into the bathroom while she put her hair in a loose bun and got some water to take her pain medicine. With one gulp she swallowed the pill and some of the water dripped down her chin. Antoine reached over and wiped it off of her chin and Brianna looked up at him with a gleam in her eye. She knew what was about to happen and fought it for so long she didn't know what to do.

Antoine leaned her up against the door and kissed her gently on her lips sucking sensually on her bottom lip.

"You never answered if I can be your man," Antoine said kissing her neck and shoulder blade.

"You just gonna fuck me and leave me. Let's just get this over with before emotions get involved and fuck things up." Brianna was confusing business with pleasure and was ready to suck his dick right there to pay off whatever debt she felt she owed him for rescuing her.

Antoine walked over to the couch and picked up the remote. He was getting angry and didn't want to show Brianna just how much he was offended by her comment.

"Let me get my shit and be out because I can already sense that shit is crazy between us. The money you loaned me will be left on the kitchen table" she said as she walked away. He was ready for her to just go but he was genuinely worried about her.

"No, don't go. Get your sexy ass over here and quit playing games." He took her hand and lead her to sit down on his lap.

"I'm feeling you Brianna but you've gotta relax and let someone take care of you. I wouldn't have you in my crib if I didn't feel anything. Bitches and niggas are always scheming but I see you ready to do whatever in order to survive."

Brianna saw the sincerity in his face and knew she had overreacted. She felt like an ass and leaned over to give him a kiss as soon as she turned his face. Their lips unintentionally met and the attraction was unmistakable. Brianna placed her hand on his back and held him close while their tongues danced a tune not heard to anyone else. Their hearts spoke all the feelings that were said for each other and skipped beats.

"Wait. Let's slow down a little before we do something we might regret" Brianna was nervous because while she had not been a virgin she hadn't had sex with someone in a long time let alone someone that she actually had feelings for.

"Wait for what? You already know I want you. Let's not play this game." Antoine reached over and pulled her closer to kiss her passionately. Their tongues danced and their temperature rose. Brianna stuck her hand under his shirt and felt his back muscles contract under her fingertips.

She took a deep breath and allowed him to walk her into his bedroom. The lights had already been dim and the Quiet Storm was playing on the radio station. 'The Neighbors Know My Name' by Trey Songz filled the room and they both felt anxious about the fact that they would be consummating their relationship.

Antoine reached over and pulled down her sweats and gripped her tight ass causing Brianna to gasp. She unbuckled his belt buckle and left it dangling. His boxers were the only thing separating them both from sexual pleasure. She didn't wear panties to bed and felt weird that she was so exposed.

He stepped out of his jeans and laid her on the bed. Antoine lifted up her leg and began to kiss slowly her pussy lips and she moaned. She had already had this done to her by Cookie but it was different this time. She actually had feelings for him and their connection was undeniable.

"Mmmmm, yes, papi!" Brianna moaned and began to run away from him but he grabbed her legs pulling her closer to him eating her pussy slowly. His lips caressed and sucked her clit making her moan loudly. His dick responded to her sounds and he wanted to enter her right then and there. He let her pussy get wetter and she twitched her leg as she had yet another orgasm. She was ready for him and he grabbed a gold wrapper from the side table and placed the barrier on his dick. He entered her slowly and she tightened up her pussy on his dick causing him to grunt loudly. With every stroke she moaned loudly and his dick grew within her.

She kissed him hard and long playing with his tongue and biting his bottom lip. He kissed her face and breasts placing her erect nipples in his mouth one by one. She became very aroused and gushed all over him. He felt himself about to lose control in her tight slit but held back.

Brianna cried out in ecstasy and wanted him deeper within her canal. He obliged and stroking harder and harder, emptied his seed inside of the latex barricade causing her to feel warmth. She moaned and kissed his face. Her wife beater was wrapped around her neck and they were both sweaty.

They spent the night getting to know each other in more ways than they anticipated and Antoine officially made her his woman despite what he knew about her dancing. He knew she didn't judge him as a dealer and didn't judge her as a stripper. That's how she made her money and they kept business and pleasure separate.

They spent an innumerable amount of time together and she became the Bonnie to his Clyde handling business for him when he couldn't do it.

Tiny became her bodyguard as well and it was easier as a woman for her to do things and get away with it. Her innocence came in handy but the question was how long would it truly be her asset and when will it become their liability.

Hide & Seek

Herman was very annoyed when he came home and didn't see Brianna there. He wanted to torture her the last few days and she wasn't around. He asked Fifi and her response was always "I don't know. This was three days ago and he still hadn't heard from Brianna after the fiasco at work. Herbie walked down the hallway to her room to see if there was any evidence of why she left and her room was as she left it. His hand was slippery with perspiration but he managed to wipe it off on his dirty blue jeans leaving a slight smudge.

Opening the door, he didn't know what he would encounter but it was worse than he ever imagined. Had he been there, he would have known it wasn't as bad as it seemed but it literally looked like a typhoon swarmed the room with Brianna's clothes and personal items thrown around the place.

He surveyed the damage and shook his head wondering what could have caused such a melee and the room in such disarray. He peeped one of Brianna's panties and slipped it into his pocket of his jeans. Herman lusted after her obsessively and he was determined to get her no matter what it would take. As he turned around to exit the room he bumped smack into Fifi who was leaning up against the column of the door watching him pine after her daughter that was chased away because of her violent behavior.

"I didn't know you had such an affinity for women's underwear! I thought you only liked how my pussy smelled on your top lip" Fifi said lighting a cigarette and inhaling the toxic grey smoke. A cloud slowly encased her head and she blew the smoke out of her ashy lips. They were so cracked they began to bleed in the creases. Fifi's hair was disheveled and she had been wearing the same clothes for days. The same

142

shirt that was bright red when purchased was now dull burgundy and the light blue jeans she once wore that was enhanced her shape was now sagging about her hips and was smudged with ashes, food and dried blood.

"Is this where your mind has been all this time? What the fuck is your fascination with my daughter?" Fifi said reaching into his pocket and removing the newly placed underwear.

"It's not what it seems, Fifi. I wanted to take it to the police to see if they can find her." Herbie reasoned with Fifi so as not to get her angry. He had already stretched the truth and they both were out of money and drugs. He was however very weak and lethargic and had no idea why. His eyes had become gaunt the last couple of days and he suffered with bouts of nausea and vomiting on several occasions. He chalked it up to fatigue, anxiety about Brianna and overwork since his job was understaffed. They both needed to find Brianna for reasons the other wouldn't disclose to each other.

"I'm a need to know why the fuck you're sniffing my daughters G-string! I mean, shit, you wanna fuck her so bad? I hear from the block she does a little dancing. Whatchu know 'bout that?" Fifi walked over and took a seat on the edge of Brianna's bed shifting it to the side causing it to fall on the floor. She had since knew what Brianna was up to but never said anything so long as she was giving her what she wanted.

"Come on Herb! I know you know! You and your fuckboys go see her and spend big money on that hoe and then come home and fuck me while fantasizing about her. I could use a good fuck right now, but your dick isn't looking so appealing without the percs." Fifi walked over and grabbed his crotch with her right hand and her left hand still held her half-smoked cigarette.

"Whatever the fuck you're doing, you need to make sure I'm high enough to not know about it. Find Brianna or else I will make sure that you won't see the light of day and your ass will house a dick bigger than yours. Trust me! You won't cum from it!" With that last statement, Fifi pushed the last of the burning cigarette into his chest causing him to cry out in pain.

The burn left a hole in his dark grey sweat shirt and began to bleed and blister. He knew he had bit off more than he could chew and he didn't know where his quest would begin but he started with the one man who seemed to have known her best- Antoine.

Bittersweet

Love, Lust & Loyalty

Brianna sat on the couch and watched Wheel of Fortune while Antoine displayed his chef skills in the kitchen sipping on a glass of Moscato. She had been with Antoine for the last three days and she hadn't been happier. Her injuries were improving and she and Antoine were getting along great.

"What did I do to deserve a man like you?" Brianna asked taking a sip of wine. "I mean I'm that 'hood bitch that ain't neva had anything good, but you have come into my life and changed it all around. I gotta ask myself if this is all real and then you lay in my arms and I feel reality tellin' me that you are."

"I'm real, baby! I'm so real every time I lay between your legs I want you to know that I'm right there making everything right. I used to fight how I felt about you but I cant. You are the woman that I've needed in my life to hold me down. So long as you don't fuck up my operations we're good" Antoine took the pasta out of the pot and finished sautéing the shrimp that was in the frying pan. He placed it on the dining table and walked over to Brianna kissing her gently on the lips.

"All I did was be there when you needed someone. That's all!" Antoine held her closer and her eyes began to water.

"You were there when I didn't want anyone but when I needed someone to be there for me"

"That's the whole point. To be there for someone when they don't want you but when they need you. That's being in love and while I can't be certain I know that you have a hold on my heart and I don't want to let you go" Antoine said with a big grin on his face. Brianna also grinned and straddled him seductively. She began kissing his neck and shoulder and giving him small pecks on his lips as he spoke.

"Now you know you're my ride or die chick right? It's you and me against the world baby! Let's get this money!"Antoine was focused on using Brianna to get the connections he needed and he knew her experience with dancing was the perfect ice breaker. She knew dancers from other clubs that would serve as escorts for whenever he wanted some out of town entertainment. Of course, he would never admit that to her but she had an idea that she was more than just an option. She was kept around for a purpose and she would soon discover why.

"Let's go away" Antoine glanced at the commercial on the TV and got the idea of a mini vacation. He had some business from a drug kingpin Paco in Miami that he had to finalize and Brianna would be a welcome distraction.

"I can't go anywhere yet. My vacation from work is almost done. I've got 2 more days and then the weekend and back to work Monday bright and fucking early." Brianna hated that she had to go back to work but she needed to make the money back that she lost and continue to save. Just because she met Antoine and they were now a couple, she was determined to still make moves on her own.

"We can go for a few days and come back in time for you to get back on the grind. C'mon Bonita! Do it for me?"

"Who the fuck is Bonita? I know you ain't just call me by no other bitch's name. That shit will get you cussed the fuck out Antoine!"

"Brianna, 'bonita' is pretty in Spanish," Antoine chuckled at her naiveté and shook his head. He ever met a woman so unpolished even though he himself wasn't what you would consider royalty. He had been with enough women to know that she needed to be refined and he was just the man to do it. As hood as he could be, put him in a suit and he would handle himself in whatever situation that arose. Versatility is what he called it and it helped him make a lot of deals that allowed him to travel to places many had only dreamed of.

"Oh! My bad!" Brianna laughed and kissed him on the lips. "So you really wanna go away with me? I ain't got no passport so where would we possibly go?"She was curious and understood that she had to allow him to take control. That was something she had a problem with because that could give him the chance to hurt her if she wasn't careful.

"Yeah I have to go to Miami to handle some business but I want you to come with me.

You down? We'd leave in the morning. I will call Tiny and ask him to book the tickets for us both and drop off the boarding pass." Brianna was getting excited for she never ventured anywhere outside of Harlem. This was becoming a dream come true and she literally pinched herself to see if it was reality.

As Antoine used the phone to make the necessary arrangements to travel the next day, Brianna sat at the table and served her dinner that her new boyfriend made. She had been with him less than a week but he was already treating her to exclusive things that she had never been privy to. Maybe she was biting off more than she could chew, she thought.

While discussing things over dinner, Antoine told her they were indeed going away and that she needed to get some things from her house in order to leave. He could buy her new clothes or she could get some from home. As much as she wanted to leave her life behind, she was drawn back to Harlem and the place that held so many memories. This time she was stronger, wiser and more fearless.

"Bonita, lets hurry up with dinner and then we'll drive by the house and get some things for you leave with me in the morning"

"NO!" Brianna didn't want Antoine to see where she lived and was worried what he would think of her family lifestyle. Knowing that someone had a drunk, alcoholic parent, is much different from seeing it in the flesh. No one knew what she was capable of and rubbing her temples which housed the recent stitches she endured she wasn't taking any chances.

"I will just go home and get some stuff and meet you back here. I won't be long, papi. No worries" she said kissing his face. She was nervous about seeing Herbie again and she for damn sure didn't want to see Fifi.

"You can't go by yourself. I will drop you off. I know Herbie is your mother's boyfriend and he's also the kinda guy I have to feed with a long handled spoon."

"Wait, so you are the one giving him drugs for my mother? Is THAT what you do? What the fuck have I gotten myself into?"

"Brianna calm down. I don't give your mother any drugs. Herbie sells my stuff to his coworkers on the side and gives me the profit. I don't mix business with pleasure so he's no friend of mine. I do keep him around because I know who will be my next client"

Brianna grabbed her clothes and began to walk out cursing herself silently for getting wrapped up in that type of mess.

"So you aren't coming with me? I want you with me Brianna. Please reconsider" Antoine was debating leaving without her but he was feeling her way too much.

"I'm going to go home and get some things. You can drive me if you feel more comfortable and then we can meet up at another time. I've gotta figure out some things and if I like being caught in the middle of your bullshit."

"You're not caught in the middle of anything Brianna. This is business and you are pleasure and until I combine the two you worry nothing about my shit. I don't worry that you shake your tits and give my pussy away because I know at the end of the day its mine"

"It's not yours Antoine. It's mine and its business for me. I simply dance for the men and they pay me for it. It's simple!"

"I rest my case Brianna. You just assumed you knew about my business and I assumed about yours. At the end of the day it's what makes us both money. Your mother is none of my concern and it shouldn't be any of my concern how you make your money. What we do is for the benefit of the other."

"Antoine, that's still my mother. She hurt me but that's the only blood family I've got. My daddy left us years ago and she's the only one that I have right now. I ain't letting no nigga come between me and her because that's family." Brianna was now close to tears and she couldn't believe she was really defending her relationship to a man she had known all of a couple of months.

Brianna gathered her things and got dressed silently. She wasn't sure what she was going to do but she needed to get out on her own because slowly her loyalties were failing around her and she had no one but herself.

"So you are leaving? Brianna, come on and I will take you and then we will go. A change of scenery will be good for us" Antoine sat on the side of the bed and put on his wheat colored Timbs and picked up his wallet and keys from the side of the mahogany dresser. The bed sheets weren't made and some of the sheets were dragging on the floor due to the sex romp they had the night before. The room still had the stench of passion in the air and Brianna wiped her face and looked back at him in sadness.

"Let's go get my stuff and when I'm done we can go. Promise me you will stay in the car until I need you"

Brianna stared Antoine in the face and made him promise to stay in the car while she got the things they needed for their little excursion. The drive to Harlem was a bit tense but they both made attempts to change the mood by playing with each other's fingers and kissing softly at various stop lights. That distraction brought them to her house within minutes and the mood totally changed. That is, until they arrived at her doorstep. Brianna's mood changed totally and she regretted what she would find.

The butterflies in her stomach expressed things and feelings that she verbally couldn't release. Fifi had hurt Brianna more than she cared to admit but then Brianna was always one to hide her feelings because she didn't like to get comfortable and then have people get close and ultimately disappear. She was afraid that Antoine would meet the same fate but just wanted to enjoy his presence for now because if he could love her at her worst, then he could love her at her best.

"I'll be fine. Thank you ,papi!" Brianna leaned over and gave her new boyfriend a kiss and ventured up the stairs to things that would change the course of her life forever. Set into motion were things that will forever change her life.

Bittersweet

When One Door Closes...

ntoine sat in the car, obedient, yet cautious about his surroundings especially since he didn't have Bear to watch his left side. He noticed some dudes watching his car and kept his hand on his Glock that was safely hidden in his waist. He stayed strapped just in case something were to pop off but thankfully never had to use it since he always had someone watching his back.

He wasn't necessarily worried but he knew that his vehicle was a target simply because of the status symbol it portrayed and caused people to question what kind of work he participated in. He kept his eyes steady on the building that Brianna entered and waited patiently for her exit while listening to music. Brianna stepped into the apartment and was greeted by the stench of a thousand deaths. She gagged so hard she almost threw up her breakfast from earlier.

"What the fuck happened here?" she said outloud not necessarily to anyone in particular. As she walked through the hallway she saw everything in the house was in disarray. She entered the kitchen and was introduced to the city rats that made themselves seen when there was food and dirt around. The garbage had been strewn all over the kitchen floor and it stunk up the whole apartment.

Brianna walked toward the back of the apartment and into the living room where she noticed her mother's olive green recliner was turned over on its side. The television had nothing but snow on it and the antenna was broken in half. Signs of a tussle were evident and it was then that she heard muffled sounds. She walked towards the sounds to find something shocking.

"Ouch!" She said, as she stubbed her toe on something. She looked down to see the body of Herbie laying there with foamy blood coming out of his mouth. Some of the blood was dried on the corners of his mouth and his eyes looked gaunt and sullen. She didn't know if she should cry or rejoice for this man was one of the main reasons why she decided to leave her mother's house.

"The muthafucka ain't dead! I wish to God he was though!" she heard a voice say. Brianna looked over to her left and she spotted Fifi with a knife in her hand. She walked over and grabbed her mother's wrist and shook it out to prevent her from causing any more fingerprints.

"Ma, what the fuck happened? Are you okay? How can you say he's not dead when he's foaming blood and laid up looking like shit." Brianna was now in a state of panic. Who knew what problem ensued and who heard what was going on before she got there.

"Calm the fuck down! He's not dead, I said, but if he is it wasn't me that killed him. I was making him a sandwich in the kitchen when the doorbell rang and he had visitors. I brought him some juice and he chugged that shit down like it was his last meal. He asked for some more and to make it sweeter. I did and came back here to cut up some cutlets and make something to eat for him and I because you know how we do when we light up. Anyway, when I came back that muthafucka was convulsing and throwing up blood and he grabbed my arm with the knife and it cut me." Fifi began to cry and held on to Brianna for dear life.

"Momma, don't be sad. I'm a call the ambulance right now and they're gonna come take him and take care of him."

Brianna took out her cell phone and promptly called the ambulance. She wondered who the visitors were that came and wanted to ask but with her mother being drunk most of the time, her caring or even knowing would be a miracle. She thought nothing of it but felt later on that it would tie into any injury sustained by Herbie. His wounds didn't look like they were simple at all and she prayed she wouldn't be caught after what she had been doing to him.

Soon thereafter, the police came as well and a report was filed with no questions asked thankfully. Fifi was able to let them know exactly what happened and they chalked it up to industrial poisoning since he worked at a place where there were toxic chemicals. Fifi waited for the morgue to come remove the body and Brianna ran downstairs to get Antoine.

"Oh shit!" Brianna said, as she ran smack into Antoine who was hustling up the steps. He

165

held her back and saw the blood on her hands and clothing and began to panic.

"Brianna, what the fuck is going on upstairs? Do I need to get back up?" Antoine grabbed his waistband to let her know he was packing his gun and wouldn't hesitate to use it to protect her.

The police came swiftly and Brianna sat on the bottom of her brownstone steps in a haze. She didn't know the last few weeks would be so eventful. Maybe she should move to Miami and leave it all behind.

"No, Antoine! Let's just go!" she said grabbing his hand and leading him away. As she looked across the street at the ambulance hauling Herbie's body into the truck she spotted Cookie rocking Prada sunglasses smoking a cigarette. She smirked at the two of them and flung the still lit stogie into the street. Smoking was a bad habit she developed when she was nervous and it showed in her face. Brianna knew that seeing her was nothing but trouble but she wasn't prepared to handle it like she wanted to. She decided to take care of it when she came back from Miami.

Antoine and Brianna made their way across the Third Avenue Bridge into the Bronx and he knew thoughts of what just happened were traveling at lightning speed through her head. He had to do something about it and quick. He grabbed her hand at a stop light and she pulled away giving a weak smile.

"I'm okay, papi. I'm just worried about my mom and I don't know what's going to happen after they find out...."

Her voice got lower when she realized she was about to tell on herself and what she did to Herbie. He deserved it though for all that he had done to her. Thankfully she wouldn't have too much more to worry about seeing as how he couldn't blackmail her anymore.

"I'm just worried about you, mami. I want you to be okay and not have to want for anything." Antoine said as he grabbed her left cheek and stroked it. He was ready to take care of her and supply whatever it was that she needed. Brianna rested her head in his hand and smiled. She felt comfortable with him and knew that she was making the right decision being with him.

Brianna and Antoine made their way onto the roads of the Bronx from Harlem and his eyes caught an elderly Spanish man on the Bronx River Parkway. There's always something going on in that area and this time it was Roses. Antoine knew this was what Brianna needed to make herself feel more comfortable about moving forward. He never knew what she was thinking and that bothered him. It was almost like she shut down so as to avoid any intense connection when she felt like she was getting too close to him. Nonetheless his plan was to gain her trust and he was going to begin and continue to do so right now.

"Abuelito! C'mere, por favor." Antoine and his broken English called the man over that had roses selling on the highway.

"Cuantos?" Antoine asked eyeing them carefully. He didn't want them to look fucked up just because they were by the roadside. He knew what quality looked like and these were extremely good looking. Their rich color and texture surpassed the fact that they were sold by a little old Spanish man.

"I give you for 12 dollars. They go for twenty but I give good price," the man replied in his thick accent. Brianna looked over with her mouth open wide and watched the transaction.

"Gimme four dozen and keep the change," Antoine said, peeling off a crisp hundred dollar bill from his wad that was kept within his personalized money clip. He glanced over and saw Brianna blushing with tears in her eyes at the long-stemmed phenomenons.

"Gracias, senor," the man said and handed Antoine the best four dozen roses that he felt money could have bought. He smiled at Brianna as she took them all in her hand and grinned. She had never been so happy in a while.

"Baby, can we go shopping for bathing suits and stuff to go to Miami in? I'm gonna need to look fly as shit if I'm going to be that bitch for you to call your own."

Antoine took a look at her and smiled, replying, "you are already my own and you are far from a bottom bitch. Let's go get my mami whatever she likes."

Brianna smiled and checked her cell phone. She had several missed calls and most of them were from Cookie. She ignored them for now but she would have to address it sooner than later. She sat back with her roses and allowed Antoine to take her wherever they needed so they could disappear from the madness that is her world. Little did she know that the moment she turned her back on Cookie, was one of the worst mistakes she could have possibly made.

On the other side of town, Cookie was at the Golden Palace smoking another cigarette, drinking a Corona, and talking to another stripper, Peaches. Peaches was a newbie that was hired once they realized that Brianna wasn't going to be back at work for a while. The place loved the chemistry between Cookie and Peaches.

"Can you believe this bitch? I been calling her for days and I go check her at her momma's house and her ass is bunned up with some chulo nigga." Cookie took a swig of beer and jumped up on the counter with her back against the mirror. She turned around slightly to examine her flowing lace front and removed a strand of hair from her face that was stuck to her lip gloss.

"Why the fuck do you care anyway? She left you in charge and you and I are making all the money that the bitch left behind. Scared money don't make money and she's as foolish as they come. I ain't tryna fuck up what I got here. I sleep all day, smoke and then come to work making money that I need. No one is up my ass and I like it. This is freedom that I neva had when I was in Connecticut. That place was so fuckin' boring." Peaches popped her bubble gum and straddled herself on the bench, reading her In Touch magazine. She spoke loudly over the music in the background which happened to be one of Cookie's favorite songs *Up All Night* by Drake.

"Are you even fuckin' listening to me? Why are you so hell-bent on that hoe and she straight flat left you! She ain't tryna get what we got. We're good! We're getting money and she's stuck out there with some bum ass dude who prolly can't fuck right and ain't for damn sure giving her as much money as we got." She was determined to turn Cookie against Brianna but she knew not that secretly Cookie was in love with Brianna and nothing could make her see wrong. She was from the old school- If she couldn't have her, no one would.

"Bitch, shut that shit up already. Me and her go way back," Cookie said, hopping off the counter and grabbing some lotion for her legs. She had to make sure her body was shining and sparkling for her next performance.

"All you need to be worried about is IF she's coming back and how you plan on taking over because you and I work well together but everyone likes how you and I operate but you can't stop Honey. She's got herself in here with regulars. Can you handle that? Can you take her regulars and show them that you are better than her?" At this point, Cookie was all up in Peaches' face, causing Peaches to jump back and look at her with a face that made her wonder what her motive was.

"What's your deal with her? You in love with her or something? You ain't gotta get all crazy 'bout her. All I said was the bitch left you. It's apparent because she's not here. She made her decision. Now YOU should decide where your loyalty lies if you want us to work on our partnership." Peaches snatched Cookie's finger out of her face and she tried to walk away, but Cookie quickly grabbed her wrist placing her at the advantage.

"Peaches, let's get one fuckin' thing straight right now. You ain't been here since the last time I popped my pussy which is often so you need to calm the fuck down and get some recognition. No one knows you yet and if they do, it's because of me. I worked well with Honey, but she bolted. That has no bearing on what the fuck your job is. Do what the fuck you are supposed to do and don't worry about anything further. I don't know why I thought your dingy ass would understand but at the end of the day it's all about money." Cookie let go of her hand leaving Peaches scared and looking into her crazy eyes.

Cookie walked out and was ready to perform and looked back to see Peaches wiping her tears. She was severely affected by what just happened but needed to recover to make the next performance believable.

Peaches was 23 and had just moved to New York from Bridgeport, Connecticut. She lived in a group home since the age of 15 and has been on her own for the last five years. The opportunity to move to New York fell into her lap and she jumped at the chance since things were not working out where she was. She began working at the Golden Palace when one night during amateur night she won $500 performing. The managers decided that she would be a great temporary addition while Brianna was AWOL. She's already been comfortable and it's only been a few days.

Peaches adjusted her signature neon orange wig and her bikini top to match. Her 40DD bosom was ample and her caramel skin shone brightly under the lights. Her eyes slanted due to her heritage of Filipino and black caused her to look more exotic than others. Her slight lisp made her appear younger than others but the one thing that made her stand out was her drive for independence.

Peaches aka Priscilla was one of those that if you pushed her hard enough she would bite back and tonight she was pushed harder than she had been pushed in a long time. She puckered up her lips in the mirror, added more mascara, kissed the mirror and prepared to go on stage to dance her ass off to her signature song *Ride* by Ciara. Her tiny waist began to forget all about the evenings troubles and she sashayed herself from behind the curtains revealing her sexual side.

She walked onto the stage and her five-inch stiletto glass heels clunked upon the recently waxed floor as she made her entrance. The music thumped in her ear drum and she squinted her eyes to see through the crowd. She noticed the men with the money in their hand ready to throw them on the stage as she performed first solo and then with Cookie. This was more important than she realized and began to grind on the shiny pole that was positioned in front of her.

Peaches took her finger and placed it in her mouth removing it only when it was moist and traced it to her bikini top that had her breast cut out and her nipples covered with tassels. She shook them and some men came to the front of the stage. She twirled around the stage and held the slippery pole tight like it was a hard penis. She thrust her crotch onto it and threw her leg around it while grinding the music. She danced a few more minutes and suddenly without warning the lights went dark and she felt a hot body near her. It was Cookie coming to join her for the rest of the performance.

Many men were cheering loudly when they witnessed Cookie enter the show. She always knew how to turn the crowd on with her fierce dance moves and seductive persona. Despite her scar on her face, she never failed to arouse all those around her and her body made up for whatever she felt she was lacking.

Her cocoa brown skin was glowing with excitement and she fell to the floor accomplishing a full split and then threw her legs over her head for effect. The crowd went wild and Peaches danced around aimlessly not yet sure of what her next move was. She felt like Cookie was taking over the spotlight which she was. Peaches was a competitive little bitch and being spoiled worked to her advantage.

She walked over to where Cookie was and pulled out her breast and began to suck it slowly causing spit to drip off of her bottom lip. Cookie's eyes lit up at her behavior and she instantly became aroused. She loved it when she was able to perform this way but didn't know she met her match and this person was worse than her.

Peaches pushed Cookie down on the floor and stood over her. She placed her pussy on her chest by straddling her and stretched out her left leg. Beneath her thigh highs held a pink rubber double sided dildo. Cookie's eyes lit up with anxiety and anticipation. She had no idea what would happen next but lay back and allowed Peaches to have her way with her. The men in the crowd went berserk! All you began to see was an abundance of money being thrown at the stage. The bartender even attempted to pay attention but had to focus on those that wanted drinks and change for dollars.

"You like to get fucked? I've got something for you!" Peaches mouthed to Cookie and placed her lips on top of hers to connect with a sensuous kiss. Cookie's pussy began to jump and she got extra wet. Peaches placed her finger inside of her mouth and then licked it slowly easing up off of Cookie. She knew exactly what she was going to do and this would teach Cookie to fuck with her.

Peaches sat on the floor in front of Cookie and began to play with her pussy. It was already moist and wet with anticipation. Peaches placed the pink dildo at the opening of Cookie's tunnel and began fucking her with it slowly. The crowd became silent with shock at what was taking place. Never had they seen anything of this magnitude take place before.

Soon the stage was filled with money of all denominations yet the women had their attention focused on each other and the pleasure they were giving. Peaches continued to thrust the phallic object deep within Cookie's canal and caused her to cum several times.

"Oh shit! Oh, my God! Oh, yeah, Yessssssssss, fuck me! Fuck me hard!" were the sounds that vibrated from Cookie's lips. She was oblivious to anyone else in the room and became a cum-chaser knowing that if Peaches continued she would squirt all over and leave a big puddle.

Peaches continuously thrust the large rubber object deep beneath Cookie's slit and she reacted with screams of a banshee making the men more aroused than they could imagine. Peaches loved the attention she received but wasn't going to abandon her pleasure for anyone else's and put her skirt up. She sat in front of Cookie and threw her legs open placing the toy inside of her also. She thrust it back and forth in and out giving mutual pleasure like none ever experienced. Whenever Cookie moved forward, Peaches moved back and they both began writhing on the stage in orgasmic bliss.

Cookie lay out on the floor with the dildo between her legs crying out in heat like a cat. Her sounds were turning the men on so much that a hush was heard amongst the crowd and everyone watched in amazement. Their faces were contorted and some of the men even had their hands in their pants massaging their well erect penises due to the visual stimulation.

"You want me to stop? Tell me you want me to stop!" Peaches was heard telling Cookie in a dominating whisper. She knew she held the cards and would not be underestimated again!

Cookie weakly gazed at Peaches and threw her head back screeching as she squirted clear liquid from her pussy hitting the neck of Peaches and splashing onto some of those closest to the stage. She braced her head back and released it all causing a puddle beneath her and a smile on Peaches' face.

The men cheered in a violent eruption of applause and threw more money at the stage. Cookie recovered and stared blankly at her new partner and Peaches looked back at Cookie in approval. She knew where she stood now and she was quite pleased with the results. Brianna's been permanently replaced as far as she was concerned and there was no stopping where and what she could do in her absence.

The NOT-So Friendly Skies

Brianna looked out of the airplane window and envisioned when she landed she would be a different person. All the shit she endured when she was in New York would be of the past. She felt like things would finally fall into place even if for a little while and she could finally be free and able to live life as it was meant to be.

Looking through the magazine's pages she saw all the things she wanted to buy but had no money to but with Antoine in her life, she knew that he would handle all of that. It was all about making her happy in his world and she was getting used to the idea. She looked over at him resting comfortably next to her and noticed his Blackberry was blinking red. He hadn't checked any messages before they took off.

Antoine shifted and the phone tumbled onto the floor leaving Brianna without any choice but to pick it up. Brianna picked up the phone and on the screen was a blackberry messenger conversation that Antoine was having with someone regarding a package that needs to be picked up at the airport. The person sent a kiss so Brianna knew it was a female. Who the fuck was he talking to and what package? Brianna felt foolish for placing any type of trust into Antoine when all he was doing was using her. She removed her shoulder from near him and that caused him to stir.

"What's up, ma?" Antoine said, rubbing her knee affectionately. He had no idea that she had checked his phone and trusted her completely even if she had. He had nothing to hide. All of his deep dark secrets were hidden deep within him in a crevice that she'd not yet revealed yet.

"Nothing. I'm fine. I'm just not in the mood." Brianna turned her back to him and looked out the window with a sullen look on her face. She wasn't looking forward to the vacation anymore and wanted to be left alone.

"C'mon. I know something is wrong. Please tell me. The next four days will determine our relationship. I want us to enjoy our time together." Antoine entwined his hand in hers playing with her fingers and reaching over to look into her eyes.

"I saw the messages on your BBM. I know about some bitch leaving you a package to pick up. I'm not fucking with you. I can't take anymore drama in my life and if you are bringing that shit to me, let me know now so you can walk away." Brianna crossed her arms over her breasts and began to pout.

"See this is what I get for fuckin' with you! You're gonna look like a real asshole when you see what I have in store for you. Keep doubting me Brianna and you're gonna lose me. That's all I have to say!" Antoine was getting fed up of the distrust and suspicions. Brianna couldn't help it though. She was subject to so much bullshit especially from her mother's boyfriends that she wanted to believe that Antoine would be that one that was different. She knew she would lose him if she didn't get a dose of act right but she also knew that in time he would walk away eventually. She was used to men leaving her after they got what they want.

Antoine and Brianna got off the plane in silence and made their way over to the luggage area. They didn't have a lot of items but Antoine was very adamant on being the first one to get their items. Two duffel bags were all they needed for their four day vacation to Miami. Anything else would be purchased courtesy of Antoine.

"Sir, would you please come with me?" a young woman came over to him saying. She proceeded to speak to him in a silent whisper giving Brianna reason to believe it was the package that she was referring to. Antoine soon came over and spoke to Brianna.

"Bonita, come with me please. They want to talk to us about something. Its apart of the surprise I had for you that you were too stubborn to believe me about."

"Papi, I'm sorry. You know I'm on edge. I promise to try to do better. That's all I can do... is try. I want you to know I am thankful for everything but I am still nervous about trusting"

"That's such a fuckin' oxymoron. How are you nervous and you bring your ass to another state with me? You know my lifestyle is

189

fucked up and what I do but I want to make a better life for us. Once I handle business here we will be done and you and I can focus on creating a better life. I'm done with the bullshit. I think I have finally met someone that I want to change for."

Brianna looked up at him with tears in her eyes and smiled. She never had a man that was so generous and kind. He was everything that she could ever ask for. He loved her despite her flaws and was perfectly imperfect and it was okay with him.

"Ma'am, we need to check your bag," a TSA agent at the airport stated to her before she was able to pass through the gate. Antoine was speaking with someone else regarding his surprise for her but she was met with a surprise of her own. Inside, they found a shoebox and pulled it out. The officer took out the shoe and gave it to the dog who kept on barking ridiculously as if he found a new toy. That set something off and Brianna looked very confused. The officer looked at Brianna with doubt and concern.

"Ma'am, can you please step into this office, please. We need to check something out," the agent said, taking her by the elbow and walking towards a back office with her bag in tow.

"My boyfriend is right there. I'm sure he can explain everything. Please! If you just let me talk to him, then I can have him explain whatever the problem is. That's not even my bag! That's his bag that I borrowed to put other necessities in."

"Sure! Whatever you say!" The TSA Agent didn't believe anything that she said and before she knew it she didn't see Antoine anymore and she was locked in an interrogation room being accused of doing something she had no idea she was guilty of.

"So you mean to tell me that you have been walking around with three kilograms of cocaine in your shoe heel and you had no idea? I'm supposed to believe that bullshit? I know we aren't as advanced as New York City, but I'm sorry. That seems to be the most absolute ridiculous thing I've heard. You must really love your man to be covering for him like this." A female TSA Officer at Miami International Airport had been interrogating Brianna for the last 90 minutes and nothing had changed as far as her reason for having the drugs. She had no idea that she could be charged as an accessory to smuggling a controlled substance and hit with jail time of up to 15 years.

"I know it looks hard to believe but I have no idea how that got in there. My boyfriend bought me those pair of shoes for our trip and I haven't even worn them. All I did was take them out of the box and look at them. I tried them on, of course, when I brought them but where the hell would I get that from? I'm not that kinda girl," Brianna began crying, trying to figure out how she was going to get herself out of this.

"Where's your boyfriend?" the male TSA agent asked peeking his head out of the office. Brianna was sure that Antoine was still there waiting on her and noticed that he disappeared. She pulled up a photo of them in her phone and showed it to the officer. He saw nothing or no one that resembled Antoine and Brianna was once again alone. It seemed every time she needed someone and was convinced that person would be there for her she was ultimately alone.

Bittersweet

Bottom Bitch

Cookie lit a Black and Mild cigarette as she walked out of the Golden Palace on a cool night. It was a nice night where the air was crisp, yet there was some heat lingering in the atmosphere. She was able to open her denim jacket and be able to enjoy the weather. It was almost 4 AM and the streets were jumping as if it was midday. She had a good night and Peaches wasn't giving her any problems. She was making pretty good money and didn't have to worry about.

"Yo, Charlene, lemme hold a dolla!" Scrappy walked over to her with a hand out and she gave him a 10 instead. She knew he was gonna use it for some weed but it was better than him getting it from someone else and ending up dead in a ditch somewhere because someone laced it with heroin.

"Scrap, when are you gonna stop smoking that shit? You know it's bad for you, but every time I see you, you got that shit rolled up and ready to smoke." Cookie stood in front of her building and took out her keys to enter. She shook her head and watched her cousin walk away. She knew within a few days she would get a phone call about him. Her child was all she cared about and to make a better life dancing was all that she knew how to do.

Cookie was in a different mindset. Scrap was her cousin and she didn't like to see family all fucked up. She had been through enough but cared only about her own because no one reached out to her to help her after her boyfriend hurt her. She still flinches when her current mate touches her but she knows they won't hurt her as she's been hurt in the past.

Walking into her two bedroom apartment in the Bronx is a far cry from the home life she

196

had before. She drops her duffle bag at the door and walks into the kitchen grabbing a Corona from the refrigerator.

"Charlene is that you?" a voice from the back emerges and it's her lover of a year. Dressed head to toe in blood red in some form or fashion was Freddie, whom she had been seeing after meeting at the Golden Palace.

"Hey, baby, yes, I am home! I missed you. I had such a long few days. I don't think that bitch, Honey, is coming back so I have to handle everything myself and make sure everyone is satisfied. I'm happy I agreed to the extra cash, but I'm sure tired of sucking old ass dicks all day. I'd rather be bunned up wit' you at night in our bed." Cookie reached over to give Freddie a kiss and grabbed a braid that hung in her face.

"Yea, well, shit ain't that easy. I gotta change shifts at the tattoo parlor so someone's gotta watch the baby and it can't be me. We'll work on it, though. I just want you to go back to working a regular job so we don't have to worry about niggas following you home. I worry when you come home and I'm not here to protect y'all. I will fuck a nigga up for hurting that sexy ass!" Freddie reached over, grabbed Cookie's plump ass, and palmed it within his fingers.

Cookie smacked the hand away and turned around to kiss her lover. She had been hurt by so many men in her life that she was tired of the bullshit that came with it. Relationships were always something that had to be negotiated when it came to men and no one understood what her job entailed. When she met Freddie, she was just looking for a friend and that's exactly what she was able to gain.

Her lips touched Freddie's juicy pink lips and she removed buttons on the red, plaid button down that was worn to reveal a white wife beater underneath. Freddie pushed Cookie slowly onto the bed and began pulling off her sneakers and jeans. She never wore underwear and that was fine because it only made access to the pussy easier. Freddie inserted a finger into Cookie's canal and began to pump hard adding a digit with every stroke. Cookie began to buck and moan loudly, gushing onto the bed and making Freddie's pussy wet and seeking some attention of its own.

Cookie never thought she would be in a lesbian relationship, but after meeting and interacting with Freddie at the Golden Palace, she decided to give it a try. It wasn't easy as she was mixing business with pleasure. Her charm was irresistible and she quickly fell hard for her. Freddie was no pushover and took control of the relationship, but respectfully. She never let anything happen to Cookie and that's what she needed and sought out after being in an abusive one previously.

"Damn, ma! You got my pussy throbbing! You need to let me fuck you before I go to work. Matter of fact, I am going to fuck you, no questions asked." Freddie was the aggressor in the relationship and while dominant, was also very polite and asked to do certain things. Their friendship was real and that's what made it such a good partnership.

Freddie walked over to the mirrored dresser in their bedroom and opened up the mahogany drawer which contained a light pink dildo strap on. Freddie removed her boxers and placed the device around her waist securing the straps around her thighs. She made sure it was tight and replaced her boxers placing the artificial penis out of the peehole. Freddie made her way to the bed and then remembered the Astroglide and brought that to the bed along with some condoms to accommodate the length and width of the dick she's taken as her own since becoming a lesbian.

"Ooooh, papi, come fuck this pussy and make it good like I know you will!" Cookie was ready and began to play with her pussy in anticipation of getting fucked by her wife.

Freddie began by hovering over Cookie's face so that the tip of the dildo rested on her lips and allowed her to begin sucking and stroking it slowly. She poured edible lube on it and rubbed it all over Cookie's lips making it shine and glisten. Cookie licked her lips hungrily and pulled her own nipples making them harden due to stimulation. This turned on Freddie even more and she eased her way down to Cookie's pussy to lick it and make it even wetter, but

Cookie resisted. She was already turned on and wanted to get down to business at hand.

Freddie placed the tip of the dildo in her moist, tight canal and began to ease in slowly. She knew in a moment, Cookie would be cumming all over the bed and she couldn't wait but for now, she was cherishing this moment. She positioned the dildo so that with every thrust it would vibrate and cause her own clitoral stimulation. With rapid movements, she strategically moved within Cookie and they kissed intensely. Cookie grabbed the back of her lover's head and turned her head from side to side as she was pushed deep within the mattress with reckless abandonment.

"Fuck this pussy , papi! Write your name on it! Shit, I love how you fuck me," Cookie's mouth said all that her body tried to express yet couldn't verbally say. Her body language coincided and she released her first orgasm within minutes, causing Freddie to also cum. Cookie gushed all over the light yellow bed sheets, causing them to look almost orange.

Freddie didn't stop. In fact, it made her work harder. She rolled Cookie over on her side and grabbed her ass, watching it jiggle. She re-inserted her plastic dick inside of her and thrust hard to bring herself to orgasm. The center of the dildo held a vibrating egg that caused Freddie to feel stimulation as well. Freddie's clit was on fire and the more she thrust within Cookie's tunnel, the more she felt herself about to have an orgasm of her own.

"Shit, this pussy is good! Damn, ma, I'm so happy this shit is all mine. Don't you give my pussy away! I will fuck you up. I'm writing my name all over this pussy. This is Freddie's fuckin' pussy, you hear me? This is MY pussy!"

"Aye, papi! Yes, it's yours. Make me cum, pa! Make me cum for you! Lemme feel your wetness!" Cookie said between thrusts and shortness of breaths. She was just about to cum and she knew that Freddie would also. It only took a few minutes for them to achieve orgasm and Freddie made sure that Cookie got hers off first.

"You ready for it, mami? Here it cums!" Freddie squirted her juices all over Cookie's thighs and began to play with Cookie's clit at the same time enhancing her arousal. She took out the dildo and began to suck her sensitive clit while placing three fingers inside of her, hitting her walls with great intensity. Cookie lost control within minutes and squirted her own juices on Freddie's tongue. They both collapsed in post coital bliss and lay in each other's arms cuddling.

"Wow; you never cease to make me feel good, baby! Thank you so much for taking the

edge off. One of the reasons why I love you!"
Cookie smiled and wiped her face on Freddie's t
shirt that was now soaked with perspiration.

"No problem, babe. I figured I hit you off
because when I go to Miami in a few days, you
will miss me." Freddie looked at her from the
side to gauge her reaction, knowing this wasn't
going to please her one bit.

"What the fuck do you mean you are
going to Miami? What's out there and why
aren't you even saying WE? You are going by
yourself? For how long?" Cookie was beyond
pissed and didn't know what she would do
without having Freddie around to come home
to. She jumped up and turned to stare at Freddie
with steely eyes.

"Relax; I will be back in a few days. My
cousin Rico is down there and needs me to
move some product for him. This is $5,000

easily. All I have to do is transport it from Miami to Fort Lauderdale and the product will be picked up by another connect to take it to Atlanta. This should take all of three days and I will be back as soon as I am done." Freddie reached over and touched her lover's face, slowly removing a stray hair. She wanted Cookie to be comfortable with the fact that she wasn't going anywhere permanently.

"Okay, okay, I guess that's fine. I just don't like to be alone and the baby misses you. I want us to be a true family now. You are all I have and I love being with you. Who will I tell the drama to with Peaches and Honey?" Cookie laughed mischievously and kissed Freddie, biting her bottom lip.

"Be careful, woman. Don't start any shit you can't finish. I leave in the morning, so let me get in the shower first and we'll go eat something." Freddie grabbed her towel and began to make her way to the shower.

Cookie waited for her lover to go into the shower and lay on the bed contemplating her next move. She didn't like that Freddie was leaving her there in New York on her own and furthermore, her story didn't seem authentic. She was interrupted by her thoughts with a vibrating sound that came from the table. Freddie's blackberry was vibrating from messages received in the pocket. Cookie went over and retrieved the phone.

"That fuckin' bitch!" Cookie said out loud and closed the phone. She never said a word about what she saw, but Cookie made sure that she kept a mental note for future use.

Home is Where the Heart Is

Brianna walked through the courtroom after being detained for two days. She hated the prison experience. Her mother was nowhere to be found which meant she was somewhere getting drunk. Of course, Herbie wasn't able to help even if she depended on it and Antoine proved himself to be just another nigga.

"Brianna Thomas, Brianna Thomas...Inmate number 284629, please come with me. Your court date is in 10 minutes," the officer said. Brianna got up from her cot in her cell and walked toward the door. She had never ever been in prison but she felt, in a way, as if she had been locked up all her life. Brianna placed her hair in a ponytail and allowed the officers to cuff her wrists with the silver shackles. Her pumpkin orange jumpsuit fit oversized on her body, but filled out the most important areas and she was teased and tormented when she walked down the corridor.

"Hey, honey! When you come back that pussy is mine."

"That pretty little face won't look the same when I'm done."

"I'm gonna pop that cherry all over my finger."

The comments continued until one of the prison guards banged the jail bars with their night stick.

"Shut the fuck up before I shut it for you!"

Walking toward the courtroom in silence, not knowing what her fate would entail, she quietly walked toward her seat and greeted her public defender who had no idea who she was but it was their job to keep her out of jail.

"Docket # 986138. The people versus Brianna Thomas," the court officer read from the manila folder immediately after the judge took her seat.

"How does the defendant plead?" Judge Vasquez said looking over the documents that would seal Brianna's fate. Brianna stood in silence and cleared her throat. She quietly entered the plea of Not Guilty. The attorney spoke his legal jargon and let the judge know that she was out of state on vacation and had no idea what transpired when the drugs ended up in her shoe. He also spoke that many items are smuggled into the airport by others and they are done, at times, by insiders. As farfetched as that may have sounded, the judge agreed to bail for $50,000 and two years' probation.

Brianna sighed in relief and as soon as she arrived in her cell, she cried for the mess she got herself into. Never did she imagine that she would be in a Florida prison fighting charges of drug smuggling. She cried until her sobs soothed her to sleep and she was awakened by keys jingling in her cell and the clanking of the door opening startled her. She sat up and wiped her eyes which were red and swollen.

"Brianna Thomas, please come with me. You have been freed to go." The officer held the door open while she hesitantly walked towards him. She didn't know what was going on, but she walked to the office for her release papers and discovered that her bail was paid for and she was scheduled to be picked up by her ride to take her back to the airport.

"Sign here and make sure we don't see your black ass back in here."

Brianna rolled her eyes and signed her name to retrieve the rest of her belongings. She replaced her name chain, hoop earrings and bracelet back to their rightful places.

"Trust me, you won't see me in this fucked up place. Thanks for the hospitality," she said, as she smiled and gave them her middle finger. They watched her plump, round ass walk away and regretted not taking advantage of her brief stay.

The sunlight hit Brianna's eyes and she looked in her purse for sunglasses. She was interrupted by the sound of Trey Songz *Say Ahh* blaring from the speakers of a car that could belong to none other than Antoine. Anger and resentment rose up in her seeing her boyfriend now; after all she's been through. He looked good, but that didn't take away from the fact that he pretty much abandoned her for the last few days without any contact or explanation.

"Are you gonna get in the car or you plan on walking back to New York?" he said, reaching over and opening the car door for her to enter. He looked at her up and down seductively because as quiet is kept he didn't want to let her go, but with her attitude and the loss of the drugs, she was now a liability and any connection to him would have been worse than she experienced already. He was saving her and she didn't know that the circumstances could have been worse than she ever anticipated.

She entered the car reluctantly and they made their way to the airport-the same place that she was caught up on charges for his negligence. Brianna kept her eyes on the highway that approached them and she decided to voice her thoughts since they had been nagging her for the last few days.

"Where the fuck were you? Why did you just leave me like that?" Antoine could hear the anger in her voice and reached over to touch her cheek. She turned her face, not wanting any contact from someone that claimed to love her but showed her otherwise.

"Bonita, you gotta know that I wanted to protect you. I did what I needed to do in order to keep you safe. They would have killed you if they knew the drugs were gone. I was able to get the money back. My cousin, Freddie, came down and we both hustled our ass off to make enough for you to get out of jail and money to get you on a plane back to New York."

Brianna looked at him with an evil scowl wanting to lash out at him. She hated the secrets that he kept from her but, because of the business he was in, she knew he had to. The bad thing was she also had secrets from him that she never told. She shivered to know what he would think if he found out she was responsible for the poisoning of Herbie. She couldn't wait to get home and resolved within herself that she would have to play his game in order to get what she wanted.

"What are we going to do? Know that I don't trust you. I want you to realize you have fucked up what we were building. How can I believe you are here to take care of me when you are not around?" Brianna sniffed trying to prevent the tears from falling from her eyes covered with the sunglasses.

"How did you get out of prison?" Antoine barked at her, waiting for a logical response. He knew she wasn't going to say anything and it angered him to even be speaking to her in that way. His feelings were so strong but this was his money and he was learning to keep it separate. The old saying goes "Money over Bitches" and his actions showed that he was all about his. Brianna wiped her face and crossed her arms as she sat in the car.

"Exactly, so shut the fuck up and know whatever I do is for your own good. I am 'bout to hit you off with $50,000 when you get to New York. If you weren't my girl, I'd not be doing this shit." Antoine looked directly into her eyes and saw he was beginning to tear up. In the short time he'd built such a strong connection with her and wanted her to feel the love he had within him. He reached over and wiped her tears giving her a strong hug.

"Brianna, I told you already that I love you and will be there for you. You have to let me help you get out of this shit that you are in. It's not beneficial. I have to get back as well but I want you home first. Let's go back to my hotel so I can give you some things to travel with as a precaution. I promise it's legal."

They traveled on the roads in Miami making their way to the Delano Hotel in South Beach; Antoine booked it knowing they would need a place to stay until their flight the next day. Brianna was skeptical but couldn't wait to take a real shower and slip into some clothes that didn't have state penitentiary embroidered on it.

She was quiet the rest of the way and Antoine wasn't mad about it. He knew what he did was wrong which was satisfy his love for money as opposed to his love for her. He did love Brianna, though, and contacted his cousin, Freddie, in the Bronx to handle some connections for him to get a ring for her. The surprise at the airport was supposed to be a proposal of sorts with the engagement ring coming later. He wanted her to move in first and then present it to her. A well-known drug lord, Ramon, fucked that up for him.

Ramon wanted payback because he found out that Herbie was working both sides, buying product from Antoine, and reselling it at three times the street price. Sadly, he was using most of it and it got back to Ramon. He sent goons to rough him up and beat the hell out of him. Fifi was none the wiser because she was drunk, but they made sure that it looked like something they brought on themselves. Brianna was oblivious that she was pretty much sleeping with the enemy.

Brianna sat in the vehicle silently staring out of the window and thought of what would have happened if she had been declared guilty of the crime. Her whole life would end right in front of her eyes. In a way, she felt obligated to Antoine and as in everything thought of ways to make it better. She felt he was taking her to the hotel room to have sex with her and remained quiet. She still wanted answers but she knew what the end result would be.

They arrived at the hotel and checked into the suite that Antoine booked. He walked around the spacious room that resembled a mini apartment with amenities that made Brianna gasp. She had never been in something so grandiose before and felt overwhelmed.

Sitting on the neatly made bed, she immediately relaxed and watched Antoine as he made necessary phone calls. She was tired and after being on a hard cot that was quite uncomfortable, regardless of the time span, being on the cozy bed made her want to cuddle up and go to sleep.

Finishing up the brief conversation, Antoine stood near the window and closed the blinds so only a bit of sunlight peeked through. The rays caught a corner of the bed and he gazed at it, not knowing where to begin with his inevitable conversation that he needed to have with Brianna.

"Brianna! We have to talk about what happened at the airport. It's important for your

safety and more so, mine. When we go back to
New York, things will be drastically different."
Antoine stood in the kitchen area and reached
into the fridge to pull out some sparkling water.
He opened the cap and placed it to his lips to
quench his severely dry throat.

With her head in her hands and tears
running down her face, Brianna gritted her teeth
and looked with blood shot eyes at Antoine.

"You left me for dead! I was in jail so you
can go running the fucking street and you tell me
that you did it for me? Fuck you! You did it for
you. You didn't want me down here with you as
company on your vacation. You wanted me to
be a damn mule for your fucking drugs!"

Antoine had no answer for that. He knew
he had fucked up and when he received a call
that Ramon's goons were at the airport, he
sacrificed Brianna, not knowing that she would

be arrested. He felt she was safer being detained in jail rather than them harming her.

"I know I fucked up! I know I risked your life. You don't think I know that? I bust my fucking ass knowing that they could have hurt you in there. I got no sleep and was worried sick."

Brianna removed her shoes and stood up, walking toward the window. She felt the hot sun beaming on her face. She went back to the very moment when she realized that she loved him and ran into his arms, catching him off guard. Passionate kisses were placed all over his face and he picked her up and placed her on the kitchen counter.

She rushed, threw her shirt over her head, tossing it in a pile on the floor. Her breasts billowed over her bra and he placed his hand beneath her underwire to remove them from their restraints. Her nipples became erect at his touch and she moaned in delight. His erection grew hearing her voice respond to his touch and they began kissing feverishly.

"Fuck me! Fuck me now!" Brianna said as she wiggled out of her pants still sitting on the cool countertop. Antoine pulled off his pants, allowing them to fall to his knees and his boxers revealed a tent that had grown from his erection that wanted to break free from the hold of his clothing.

He grabbed a condom quickly out of his wallet, placed it on his dick, and brought her waist forward to meet his. He slowly guided her on top of him and she began to buck immediately at feeling him deep within her. With the counter leveraging most of the weight he was able to pummel her deep and his knees hit the cabinets with each thrust.

Harder and harder, he remained inside of her and they both moaned incessantly with sweat dripping off of their bodies. Antoine picked her up, still embedded in her throbbing pussy, and carried her to the bed where he laid her on her back and fucked her deep.

"Oh, my God! I love you!" Brianna moaned between breaths and kissed him slowly with her tongue dancing a tune only they both heard within their hearts. She knew this was make up sex and she told him to fuck her, but they were indeed making love and he stroked her deeply, with his eyes closed praying silently that this feeling would never end.

"I'm sorry, bonita. I'm so sorry," Antoine admitted to her and his pace quickened. The more he apologized was the more he realized that this may be the last time he would make love to her. What if he lost her, he thought to himself. He couldn't bear for that to happen and the harder he slammed into her pussy, causing his balls to bounce on her ass and clit. She shivered and gave indication that orgasmic bliss was near. He buried his face in her neck and grunted for what seemed like forever as they both reached climax simultaneously. Left sweating profusely, they lay in each other's arms and drifted off to sleep.

Meanwhile in another part of Miami

"Where the fuck is my money? "drug king Ramon asked Freddie, Antoine's cousin as he waves around a machete' to torment her. Freddie whimpered through the silver masking tape that covered her mouth. Her ebony hair was matted with blood and her light face was bruised and battered from the physical torture they put her through. Even though she was the appointed male counterpart in her relationships, her bravado was no match for her captors.

"Yo, let's just kill the bitch and do away with her. Ain't like she's speakin' anytime soon," Eazy said. He was one of Ramon's henchmen and he garnered that name because killing people was very easy for him. Once when money was owed to Ramon, he followed the man to his residence and waited quietly until he was asleep. He barged in during the wee hours of the morning and stood over the man, listening to him beg for his life.

Tired of hearing his pleas he removed the pillow from behind the man's head. He covered his victims face with it, took out his Glock 9 and placed it on the pillow releasing a single shot to his victim's forehead, ending his life instantly.

"Not yet, Eazy!" Ramon said in his heavy Spanish accent. He stared into the pleading eyes of Freddie whose white wife beater was stained with her own blood.

"Where the fuck is my money? You better tell me or else we will be sending a message to your little girlfriend that her boyfriend is gone," Ramon said while walking toward Wild, his other henchman. He was more the perverse type and looked lustfully at Freddie, knowing exactly what he was going to do.

"Boss, what are we gonna do? Are we gonna do away with this dyke bitch or are we gonna keep her around for collateral?" Wild said. He walked over to Freddie and ripped off her wife beater, leaving her in nothing but a sports bra. Her fear caused an erection and that was exactly what he wanted to happen.

"I don't give a fuck what y'all do, but keep her around and alive. I need to send something to send to Antoine as a message. Do it expeditiously and send it to the Delano Hotel, then have your way with her." Ramon casually waved his hand dismissing his henchmen from his presence and exiting the dungeon like room where he kept Freddie captive. She had been there for two days and they had done so much damage to her that her eyes were swollen shut from the constant friction. Her dried tears stained her face leaving her rosy lips cracked and dried.

Eazy and Wild were handsome men, but not Freddie's type obviously, and when they found out she enjoyed the female persuasion, they found every way possible to torture her and make her feel like less of a person. They had already raped her repeatedly, leaving her female parts battered and bruised. She cried during every stroke as she couldn't move her hands which were tied above her head. She was bent over the cold metal chair and positioned so they could enter her from the back. Once, they even fucked her in the ass and pussy at the same time, leaving her ass hole raw and blistered.

"I ain't in the mood to fuck, but I am kinda horny from seeing her all tied up and shit," Wild said. His dark Caeser waves shone in the spotlight that was the only thing illuminating in the room.

"What the fuck is your problem? Let's just off this bitch. I'm tired of tending to her ass. She's taking up way too much of my time." Eazy was getting frustrated and it showed. He held up a small hunting knife and walked over to Freddie holding it to her neck. He moved it down her shoulder and traced it to the outside of her left arm. He dug the blade deep into her shoulder, digging into her flesh.

"Ahhhhhhhhhhhhh," Freddie was heard saying beneath the tape used as a gag to silence her. Wild stood over her watching this whole ordeal and laughed sadistically. He noticed in the corner was an empty match box and held it in his hands. He knew what Eazy was going to do and was waiting. Eazy dug into her skin and carved out a piece of her flesh that contained tattoo which said "LOCA" under a cross covered in barbed wire.

Blood splattered all over his shirt and dripped onto the floor as Freddie tried to move to ease the pain, but couldn't because of the restraints. Once finished with removing the bleeding flesh, Eazy passed it to Wild who placed it into the matchbox and handed it to him.

"This should make Ramon happy; the bitch is alive, but we have the message to send to Rico," laughed Wild. Seeing all that blood and seeing her cry made his dick rock hard.

"Ayo, Eazy, go give that to the boss while I talk to her for a minute."

"Don't do anything crazy. We still need her to be alive." Eazy wasn't one to follow orders unless it benefitted him and he hated when Ramon was pissed with him.

"Nah, I'm good. I just need to relieve this pressure, you know what I'm saying. I don't think I'm in the mood to have you looking at my dick today," Wild laughed and opened his zipper as Eazy walked away to give Ramon the souvenir he requested.

Wild stood in front of Freddie and began to taunt her with his dick. She attempted to turn her face away, but he made it very difficult. He ripped off the tape to mask her sounds and stuck his dick in her mouth. She resisted, but realized that the more she sucked, the more he would possibly do what she asked; the saying goes, one hand washes the other.

"Yea, you dyke bitch. I knew I could convert you. Suck this fat dick like your life depends on it," Wild said, fucking her face slowly. Freddie spit on his dick and in her mind imagined it was Cookie's pussy that she was licking and sucking. She envisioned that her clit grazed her tongue ever so slightly and that she was tongue kissing her pussy making her shiver and cum like she often did when they made love.

Wild grabbed the back of her head and fucked her face harder, making his dick touch the back of her throat. Sucking harder than water down a drain, Freddie relaxed her throat and took Wild's entire dick in her mouth and deep throated him.

"Oh, shit! Oh yeah, baby. Take this dick! Take it like a champ!" Wild was enjoying himself and felt his dick throb with an anticipated orgasm. His dick trembled within her throat and she believed he was about to cum. She began to move her mouth off of his dick, but he pushed it further and shot his sticky wad down her throat. Freddie's eyes bulged at the taste and texture of semen that she'd never been exposed to. Wild smiled and removed his now flaccid member out of her mouth.

"You suck a mean dick! Don't let anyone tell you different," he said, laughing while cleaning himself up with a dry piece of tissue he had in his pocket.

He shook his head and chuckled, "I can't believe you're wasting those sexy lips on pussy." Wild shook his head and continued to clean up, bending down to wipe her face that was still sticky from the blow job while smirking.

"You know, you could be more nice to me. I did feed you. Maybe if you get out of here alive, I could make you my bitch," Wild whispered closely to her face, but before he could move, he was greeted by vomit.

All the contents of her stomach which was mostly bile, water and semen was released unto Wild's face and he was not happy at all.

"YOU NASTY BITCH!" Wild took out his gun and used the butt of the gun to pistol whip her in the face. Just when he was done, he cocked the gun and was about to end it all for her, Eazy walks in and stops him.

"Wild, no! What the fuck are you doing? What have you done? Awww man, you fucked up now for real! Ramon isn't going to be happy. She's half past dead, man. Bitch can't even open her mouth or eyes to tell us where the money is."

"Fuck that hoe. She's only as good as her pussy and I had that and don't want it no more. You can off her as far as I'm concerned. Disrespectful bitch! Since when has your ass gained a conscience, anyway? You're the first muthafucka to shoot first and ask questions later."

Wild walked toward the door and went to get himself cleaned up. He was pissed, but laughed about it as he ran up the stairs. Something wasn't right with Eazy and he was going to find out why he was being so nice to Freddie.

"Why...did you...save me?" Freddie said through her swollen lips. Blood gathered in her mouth and she spit it on the floor beneath her. She was ready to give up, but Eazy gave her promise to hold on.

"Don't talk. I gotta get you safe for the sake of momma and papa. I can't believe this is the life you've chosen. I haven't seen you in seven years. I can't believe my little sister is a lesbian!" Eazy loosened the ropes around her wrists and wiped the blood from her lips lovingly.

Just at that moment Wild returned from seeing Ramon and made his way back to the makeshift dungeon so he could finish punishing Freddie. Behind the door, Wild cocked his pistol, awaiting the moment when he would have to use it in the event of a betrayal. He knew blood was thicker than water but the taste of blood was always much sweeter.

The Rotten Apple

rianna made her way up the brownstone steps and looked back at Antoine. She didn't have the time that she expected to have with him, but their relationship absolutely changed and was cemented for the better. She failed to recognize the car double parked in front of her home and was met with surprise as she saw two detectives sitting with her mother in the living room.

"Brianna! I didn't know you were coming back," Fifi caught herself and rephrased her statement. "I thought you would be back in another day or two," she said, while getting up to give her daughter a hug. Brianna reacted stiffly after the altercation that transpired before she left and saved face in front of the police. She had enough of law enforcement trying to get involved in her life the last few days and wanted to know why her mother was being questioned.

"No, Momma. I said I would be back sooner. You must not have gotten my message. Is everything okay? Why are the police here?" Brianna dropped her bags and stared at them inquisitively trying to feel out the vibe in the room.

"Ms. Thomas, we are here regarding the death of your mother's boyfriend, Herman. He passed away yesterday in the hospital and the autopsy revealed this morning that, while he had suffered some type of poisoning, he was also beaten. The drugs in his system enhanced the bleeding causing him to lose blood faster and therefore expiring. The medication in his system was warfarin along with dosages of strychnine. The combination tore the inner lining of his heart, making it weak. The beatings he obtained were the end result, causing his inevitable death."

"Oh my!" Brianna feigned discomfort and sadness knowing that she was involved in the poisoning. The beating was his own doing and frankly, she felt after what he used to do to her by torturing her mentally and sexually, he deserved it. It was only a matter of time before it caught up to him. The detective looked at Brianna and eyed her suspiciously, so she turned her head away.

"Ms. Thomas, your mother tells me that you are a nurse. Would you have any access to these products found in his system? And would you have motive to want him dead? I understand you and him didn't have such a good relationship and argued often. Your mother also said he was partially the reason why you left to go on vacation. Here's my card." The detective stuck his hand into his blazer pocket and pulled out a business card with his phone number and email address. He handed it to Brianna, still eyeing her suspiciously, and she began to fidget nervously.

"Thank you, sir. I will be sure to contact you with any information that I may have regarding this issue. I'd like to speak to my mother privately and proceed with the funeral arrangements while we await the call from the hospital." Brianna held her mother close continuing the façade of the concerned daughter, when she couldn't wait to light into her ass for all that's taken place. This has been the craziest few weeks she had experienced in her life and was hoping that soon she would be able to happily say it was over. The butterflies in her stomach told her otherwise.

Brianna and her mother showed the detectives out of the house and proceeded to the kitchen where Fifi sat and had a cup of coffee to calm her nerves. Knowing that wasn't enough she got up and pulled out a flask of brandy from the kitchen cabinet to toss into her mug. She took a big gulp and began to relax now that the cops were gone. Brianna used this as the moment to confront her mother about all that had been taking place.

"Momma, what the fuck has been going on since I have been gone? How did the cops even know about my trip and what did you tell them?" Brianna was furious and Fifi looked at her in a fit of rage. After last time, she knew better, though, than to react in such a violent manner. Her being alone showed her that she needed Brianna more than she could ever have imagined.

"Brianna, I didn't tell them anything; I promise. I don't even know how they knew where we lived. I do know they mentioned if you knew anyone by the name of Charlene and I said no. They said you work with her. I had never heard of you speak of anyone with that name, so I just agreed. We gotta get them off of our trail because they will find out that Herbie was giving me drugs and I can't lose my money over that shit. I can't go to jail!"

Listening to Fifi caused Brianna to blank out and all she could think of was when she saw Cookie across the street one particular day. Somehow, she knew she would have to face her and she had been avoiding her until she got herself together. Now Cookie brought her bullshit to her front door, so she would have to step to her face to face. She hated going back to work there especially when she didn't have to, but it was the only way.

Watch the Throne

The music of 2Pac's *How Do You Want It* blared through the speakers of The Golden Palace and while it was great to be back in a familiar place, Brianna dreaded going back there.

"Yo! Is that my girl, Honey?" Bear said, as he removed the crimson rope and let her inside a restricted area of the club.

Seeing a familiar face calmed Brianna's nerves and she was happy it was Bear. She reached up to embrace him and gave him a juicy kiss   on   the   cheek.

"Bear! How are you doing? I am so happy to see you. It's been only a few weeks, but so much has changed. I had to take a leave of absence from work and I heard I was replaced on my set with Cookie. How is she?"

Bear's face said it all. Things were not working out as they thought and when he finished filling her in with the information, Brianna was stunned. She never thought things would be out of control like that but in retrospect, anything was possible when dealing with greed and Cookie had a lot of it.

"Peaches and Cookie are in the back doing what the fuck they do best. You have no idea what's been going on since you left! I'll let you judge for yourself." Bear gave Brianna a kiss on the cheek and shook his head. He had wanted to tell her, but she needed to see for herself what had erupted all in the name of greed.

Brianna took a step into the locker room and said hello to some of the other girls. Her attention was focused on the two girls in the back, laughing and chuckling. She almost didn't recognize Cookie, but the scar on her face gave her away. Her complexion had gotten a tad lighter and her breasts were doubled in size.

"Who the fuck is this bitch and what is she looking at?" Peaches leaned over the table that held a razor blade and several grams of cocaine lined up on a mirror. Things had taken a turn for the worse and Brianna felt responsible. In retrospect, she was the one that initiated everything and prompted Cookie to do all the things she was currently involved in. Cookie never would have done all of those things if Brianna wouldn't have told her and shown her how much money was involved in doing so. Money was truly the root of all evil.

"Well, look who decided to drag her tail back to work." Cookie sniffed a line and placed her hair behind her ears to keep from getting in her face. She looked Brianna up and down with eyes that resembled daggers. Cookie wiped her nose and took a gulp of Hennessy that she had next to her. The drugs and alcohol turned her into a totally different person and Brianna began to have feelings that this wouldn't end well.

"Hey, Cookie, how are you? Long time, no see." Brianna took a seat by one of the makeup tables and placed her pocketbook on the counter behind her. She placed her hair in a ponytail and looked at Peaches, who seemed ready to pounce as soon as Cookie said the word.

"I'm chillin'. You know how we do. Making money and eating pussy. Whatever gets me through the day." Cookie erupted in laughter and slapped Peaches with a high five.

"Cookie, I'm a just cut to the chase. What the fuck did you tell the police why they came to my house? My mother was worried sick and I kept getting looks from the cop. I don't like to be put on the spot, especially since I just came back from vacation." Brianna was getting annoyed and ready to fight. Blood boiled within her veins and anger rose up in her. She rose up and grabbed Cookie by the neck.

"Bitch, what the fuck do you think you are doing? You think you gonna take me down like you did Herbie? I know you are just like your father. You've got murderer running through your veins," Cookie began rambling and Brianna had no idea what the hell she was talking about.

"Yo, Cookie, you want me to call for back up?" Peaches hopped up and approached Brianna, ready to fight, but she was too high to really do anything. She and Cookie had been drinking for hours waiting for their set and she could hardly function, let alone fight.

Brianna rolled her eyes and took a look at Peaches, Cookie's new little minion and shook her head. Cookie wasn't about to back down from Brianna especially since it was her doing that created the monster that she had become. She nodded at Peaches and said "Let Bear know I'm back here with this bitch and we will be on later, if at all. Her and I have some unfinished business to tend to."

Peaches handed Bear some money and he shook his head to show he understood and would leave them be. He was still being paid under the table and enjoyed it, but he wasn't about to allow Cookie, someone who he had no real loyalty to, to hurt Brianna, who hooked up him lots of times and he actually cared about her. Bear jumped on the phone and made a phone call quietly while the girls chatted loudly.

"Boss, its Bear. Yeah I'm at the GP. Something's about to go down and you need to protect her. I've done my best, but she just came back today and is kind of upset. No, I didn't tell her. I'm leaving that up to you. Okay, see you then." Bear hung up the phone and stood within eye shot of where Brianna and Cookie were. He listened out for his boss' appearance as well, because he knew this would affect everything, whether it is positively or negatively.

"Bitch, do you know what the fuck I've done for you? Who are you to threaten me? You got me fucked up with someone else. Don't act like you know me and don't act like you know my daddy! Are you crazy?"

"Yeah, bitch, I know about your momma and your daddy. I found out why your momma began her drug problem. Your mother's such a fucking slutbox that she can't keep her legs closed and got caught sucking off a dude from your block. His wife beat the shit out of her and that's how Fifi gained her reputation. You think that she was well known because of her pretty face? You are sadly mistaken and dumb as a bag of rocks if you do believe that bullshit."

Brianna's mouth dropped hearing about her mother's past from someone else. She reached up and slapped Cookie so hard that she popped a blood vessel in her finger. Cookie reached over and grabbed Brianna's ponytail and they began fighting and writhing around on the floor. Brianna held Cookie down and began punching her without remorse in her face and about her body. Cookie endured a bloody lip, but kept on fighting trying to gain the upper hand. She got some licks but was off balance because she was intoxicated.

"You fucking bitch! I actually thought you were my friend. How could you talk about me and my momma like that?"

"Brianna, it's easy! Your mother is a slut just like you; that's why your daddy left! He couldn't take it anymore. Your mother is a slutty bitch, Brianna, and so are you! Your precious boyfriend will know how much of a hoe you are and how you eat pussy for money."

At that moment, Antoine walked in and heard that last part that was said. His mouth dropped and he was met with stares of shock. Brianna began pummeling Cookie with punches and slaps but couldn't do too much more damage as Antoine came over and scooped her up while her arms flailed aimlessly.

"Get the fuck off of me! She's tryna tell me that my mom is a hoe and I'm not believing it. She ain't got no right to be talkin' shit bout my momma."

"Bitch, please! I have every right. She ain't exempt. I wish I never met your trifling ass. You got me caught up in so much shit. Tell me why the fuck I got a box filled with my girlfriend's tattoo! Y'all muthafuckas got her killed! I hate you!" Cookie lunged at Brianna, but Antoine stepped in between and spoke up.

"Cookie, who is your girlfriend? What does she look like and what does she have to do with this?" Antoine looked closely at Cookie and realized he was staring right into the eyes of Freddie, his cousin.

"Aye, yo! Is your girlfriend Freddie? She told me her girlfriend's name is Charlene. You don't even look the same like in the picture that she showed me."

Cookie walked over to Antoine and spit in his face. Antoine lunged at Cookie and Brianna stopped him, wanting to get to the bottom of this. This was becoming a little too crazy. How was everyone all ofa sudden involved with one another? T*alk about six degrees of separation*, she thought to herself.

"Cookie, I mean Charlene, I had no idea that Freddie was your girlfriend. I didn't even know you really got down like that. I thought it was only for show and money." Antoine peeled off 10 crisp, hundred dollar bills and gave them to Cookie. She looked right at the money and threw them back at him.

"You think I want your fucking money? My girlfriend is out there, probably dead, and you give me a thousand dollars? What the fuck am I gonna do with that shit? I make a thousand dollars in 10 minutes. I don't need your fucking money. I had to make do with what I had to without it. My kid and I are surviving without Freddie. I had to make enough money for us and used a little extra for myself," she said, as she pushed up her boobs in her bra.

Brianna stepped up and in Cookie's face and started to rationalize the situation and realized that Cookie fell in lust with her.

253

"Is that why you hate me so? My boyfriend is involved in your girlfriend's disappearance? Do you know what the fuck I've been through? I've been to hell because of you You were the one that told the police about me, didn't you? I saw you across the street when they took Herbie's body away. You told them I killed him. I didn't kill him. He killed himself. All the shit he did to me and my mom, he deserved to die. If I had to do it again, I would have. I hate him for everything he's put me through. He took my momma away from me and she's all I have. I ain't got no daddy to love me..."

At that very moment, Ramon, Eazy and Wild walked into the Golden Palace and all was silent.

Sweet Vengeance

Ramon, Eazy and Wild walked into the Golden Palace and were ready for confrontation. They had been contacted by Bear who let them know that a potential altercation was going to take place.

"Rico, please tell me these bitches aren't fucking with my money. I've invested way too much and I refuse to have it all be a waste of my time as this is my establishment. You know what we do and I won't have this be the reason why my money is funny."

Antoine stepped up and approached his boss to let him know all is well.

"Nah, Ramon, you are good. Don't worry about it. I am just handling some personal shit that I had no idea I was involved in."

"Rico, business and personal doesn't mix. Tell the bitches to get back to work so my money can be made. I believe in multiple cash flows just like I believe in multiple pussy. A lack of any will cause me to be very unhappy. You don't want me to be unhappy. If I am not happy, then I will make your life a living hell."

Just then, Cookie walked forward and whispered to Brianna something that would cause her to turn around and slap the shit out of her.

"There's your daddy, bitch! Say hello!" Cookie cackled loudly, until Brianna literally slapped the taste out of her mouth and she fell to the floor with Peaches running to her aid. Eazy and Wild tried to grab her, but she wiggled out of their grasp.

"There seem to be a problem?" Ramon walked over to Brianna and took a look at her.

He never saw her, but when their eyes locked, it was as if they were looking into a mirror.

"Who is your mother?" Ramon wiped the tears from Brianna's cheek and told his goons to give him a minute. He never allows anyone to get too close to him, but he didn't feel threatened by Brianna.

"My mother is Fifi," Brianna responded quietly through tears.

"Ophelia from Harlem? She's your mother, right? I remember her. You favor her when you make certain facial expressions. I see it when you are upset mostly."

Ramon turned to Cookie and asked Eazy to help her up. He grabbed her by the neck and looked her in her face. Wild stood right beside Ramon just in case anything popped off. He was ready as well because he didn't know what would possibly happen.

"How did you know that Brianna was my daughter?" The gasps heard behind them were unmistakable. Antoine grabbed his head between his hands and looked at everyone in shock and amazement.

Cookie remained stone faced and didn't answer, so Ramon asked the question again. "How the fuck did you know that Brianna is my daughter, bitch?"

Cookie looked at him and said, "The streets are always watching. When you are raised by the streets, you listen to what it has to say, whether you ask the question or not."

"Wrong answer!" and Ramon nodded his head and Wild shot Cookie directly in the forehead leaving her in a crumpled, bloody heap.

Antoine grabbed his gun and took aim at Wild and Eazy who also responded with their weapons aimed at his head.

"What the fuck you do that for? How can you get any answers if you kill her?" Antoine was confused, but Ramon called him over.

"I don't need that bitch to tell me how she knew. I'm quite sure she found out through some text message or some email. I keep tabs on everyone's electronic devices. I also know that you are in love with Brianna. I know that your cousin, Freddie, was caught up in the whole mess. I'll return her dead or alive when I am done with her and not a moment sooner. 'Til then, clean this mess up."

"Ramon, am I really your daughter? Why did you leave me and my momma?" Brianna couldn't not ask the question that she had been dying to ask. Finally, she would get her answer and things would change. Ramon's eyes softened as he looked at the person who he had been looking for all these years and when he stopped, found her in a most unlikely spot.

"Yes, Brianna Marisol Thomas, you are my daughter. Your mother and I were together long before you were born, but I was a young man caught up in the drug game; back then, crack was hot on the block and I wanted to be a boss. The problem was that everyone knew she was my lady, but she didn't care. She never represented me as if she was the First Lady and did all sorts of reckless things. Granted, I know that I was selling rock but I was earning respect for it. She began messing around behind my back with a rival drug lord and I caught her sucking his dick behind my back." Brianna wiped the tears from her face and listened closely, as she realized Cookie was indeed telling the truth. He continued with his story and she

could see he hated reliving the past, but it was
the only way to approach a future.

"The rumors followed soon after that she
was pregnant with his baby. She had no idea who
the father was because she was such a slut and I
ended up leaving before she had you. Your
mother kept me from you and I had no way of
keeping in contact with you. I connected with
another drug lord in Florida and he was my
uncle, Tito. He taught me the business before he
died and I have been doing it for the last 22
years as one of the biggest. No one wants to ever
fuck with me or get into my way. I have some
top clients that are celebrities, men of power,
and the best lawyers."

"Even if I am arrested, or one of my
people are arrested, I bail them out. I had no
idea that you and Antoine were involved, but I
gave him 50grand on the strength that it was
family. Herbie was working for me also and he

was fucking with our money. He was playing both sides and I don't like when people do that. I can't trust you if you are smiling in my face and fucking me over behind my back. I will not tolerate that."

Anger rose in Brianna also and she lunged after Ramon, beating him about his chest, crying out because of the betrayal she endured. For years, she knew nothing about her father and suffered mistrust from several men because of it. She exploited herself all because she wanted to get out of her situation and did it by any means necessary.

Wild and Eazy grabbed Brianna and tried to remove her from Ramon.

"No! Don't hurt her!" Ramon cried out. It was too late as Brianna grabbed the gun and shot Ramon square in the heart, leaving him shocked and gasping for air. Bloody matter flew onto the floor and his goons were in shock. They went for their pistols also and Antoine reached for his to protect his love.

Gunfire was heard everywhere and when the smoke cleared, no one was alive. Brianna lay on Antoine's chest with a single shot to the temple and Antoine's body was riddled with bullets. Eazy and Wild's bodies were riddled with bullets that were released from Antoine's gun before he met his doom. All was silent in Harlem and Brianna and her father were reunited in both life and death. She finally received the escape that she needed to get out of the slums of New York City. It wasn't how she wanted but she got it.

"Hello? 911! I'd like to report a shootout. Yes, there are several bodies. Yes, I am here waiting. My name is Peaches."

PROLOGUE

"Ms. Ophelia Thomas?" a gentleman
with a dark suit and wire rimmed glasses
approached her as she sat in a mahogany chair in
a lobby. She was dressed in a dark blue skirt with
a matching blazer. Her hair was in a ponytail and
her white blouse was buttoned to the top and
revealed an antique cameo.

"Mr. Walters, it is so nice to meet you
however it's sad that it has to be under these
circumstances.

They both were lead into the office and
Fifi looked into the manila folder that was
presented to her and signed a form. It was an
insurance check made out to her in the form of
five million dollars. Ramon Sanchez knew that
his life would end the way it began and while he
believed that Fifi was a slut, he knew within his
heart that Brianna was his daughter. He placed a

life insurance policy on his life and hers and made Fifi the beneficiaries in the event of their untimely deaths. Unbeknownst to her, her time was coming as well, for he placed a cost on her life, too.

"Thank you very much, Mr. Walters. This will come in handy as I recover from my losses and begin my new life."

Fifi smiled and walked out of the office with the check snugly placed in her pocketbook. While walking down the stairs, she bumps into a woman and apologized promptly.

"I am so very sorry as well. Have a great day!" she says has she walks into the building that Fifi just left.

"Mr. Walters, there's a young woman here to see you."

"Hello. Mr. Walters, my name is Peaches... um, I mean, Priscilla. It is very nice to make your acquaintance, sir."

"What brings you here?" Mr. Walters said, taking a seat behind the desk.

"I'd like to speak to you about the estate of Ramon Sanchez and Alfreda Martinez, otherwise known as Freddie," she said with a smile.

"Yes, I am familiar with them. Situations like that are often so bittersweet," he said, while going through his paperwork.

"Yes, they are sir... they certainly are," she said.

THE END